All the
Best xo
M Tasia

SHAW

Fire Lake – Book 3

M. Tasia

ALSO BY M. TASIA

The Boys of Brighton series

Gabe

Sam's Soldiers

Rick's Bear

Jesse

Coop

Travis

Grady

Vincent

Shadow

The Holidays

The Gates series

Saint

Finn

James

Joey

Bradley

Carlos

Sawyer

Trey

Fire Lake series

Brick

Fletcher

EVERYONE LOVES THE BOYS OF BRIGHTON

"I loved this book and I love this town. I hope there's going to be more."
—Melissa Lemons on *Gabe*

"An amazing read that was filled with lust, love, crazy hot sex, danger, action and so much more This is the first book I have read in this series but I will definitely be reading more in the future."
—Gay Book Reviews on *Sam's Soldiers*

"I was crazy impressed that the author made me teary over the ending of a relationship that I shouldn't have even been invested in. I didn't yet know these characters yet the author made me hurt for them. That takes some mad writing skills!"
—Love Bytes Reviews

"Jesse and Royce together have my heart. Jesse has it all by himself."
—The Book Junkie Reads on *Jesse*

"So much action, intrigue, drama and angst for the long awaited story of Grady and Ben. This was worth the wait. Sexy and sweet. I can't wait for the next."
—SamD on *Grady*

"I knew this one would be my favorite to date! There was something about Vincent that said awesome then came Tristan."
—Booky on *Vincent*

"This installment of the Boys of Brighton was so good! I loved Shadow and Randy 's story I was hooked from the first page to the last. This book was definitely worth the wait!"
—AG on *Shadow*

"I have loved this series from the very first story and this holiday novella is simply perfect. We get a glimpse of all our couples and what is happening in their lives while the holidays explode around them. I cannot wait for more!"
—bookobsessed on *The Holidays*

ANOTHER BIG LOVE – THE GATES

"Ms. Tasia has done it again! This is Saint's story, for readers of the Brighton Boys, you'll know he needs a break! After being forced to become a plastic surgeon by his father, he rebels by assisting people in 3rd world countries, which puts him in the position to be kidnapped and tortured. You really feel for him, that's for sure! Max is the perfect man for poor Saint's battered soul, not that he doesn't have his own issues! Overall, this was engaging, steady paced and chock full of all the feels!"
—Avid Reader on *Saint*

"Finn and Miguel stole my heart. This is a great Sunday afternoon read. Finn's character jumped off the page as his story developed through each chapter. I loved reading his truth and watching him and Miguel find their home in each other."
—K.A. Brown on *Finn*

"This is really a great series and I def recommend it. I loved James and Ross, it was a rough start for the two, but they worked it out. I can't wait for more, love everything M. TASIA writes!"
—TammyKay on *James*

"I may have my new favorite book couple of the series. Joey and Sam just have that something special. At one point I was ugly crying but it was a good ugly cry if that makes any sense. I really love the series and I can't wait for her next installment!!"
—Vine Voice on *Joey*

"This author is really talented and I love her series, this one and the Boys of Brighton. Her characters are so well drawn and I can really get into the stories. I especially loved Eric in this particular book. I'm hoping Clay the rookie will be the next book. Keep 'em coming!"
—Rosemary on *Bradley*

"Two men with damaged souls come together and find love. A tried and true formula that works well here, especially when working with two lovable characters like Carlos and Clay. Carlos especially was interesting to me - the contrast of his appearance to his gentle nature, a true gentle giant. And Clay being all protective of the much larger, but more gentle man - so sweet! I really liked this story and am looking forward to more of The Gates now."
—Valeen on *Carlos*

"Sawyer is the newest addition to The Gates series. The book is very emotional, sweet, funny, romantic, and these two are great together. I look forward to every book in this series."
—Elaine Gray on *Sawyer*

"This book has all the feels and pulls the reader right in. It was wonderful to see how the two of them went from adversaries to respect to falling in love. You won't want to miss their story to see the path they travel and if there is a HEA waiting at the end. There is much more going on here, but hopefully this is enough to convince you that you will not want to miss this one."
~Emily Pennington on *Trey*

READERS ARE WILD ABOUT FIRE LAKE

"What a great beginning to a series! Brick and Roman are perfect together. Add in the murder factor and some well trained military men and you have the makings of an awesome series. It was a well written story that kept me engaged from the first page. Cannot wait for Fletch, Spencer, and Shaw's book."
~I Love Books 2005 on Brick

"Fletcher is the latest in M. Tasia's Fire Lake series, a lineup of action-packed M/M romances that I LOVE. Fletcher Daniels is a retired Navy SEAL - handsome, brave, and loyal to the military brothers with whom he has formed a security company, and he finds himself drawn to the local sheriff. Elias Cooper is as sexy as he is protective, and he wants Fletch just as much. Just when they decide to see where this burning attraction will lead them, the new couple, along with Brick and the other guys, become immersed in a missing persons case that hits really close to home. Fletch and Elias are equally strong, passionate men with their own demons, and it makes them one hell of a fierce couple. The respect with which Tasia treats these super steamy love stories gives me all the feels, and those heart-tugging aww moments, the sexy bits, and the suspense make it REALLY difficult for me to wait for the next installment. Once again, such amazing work, M. Tasia!"
~Shannon Williams on Fletcher

www.BOROUGHSPUBLISHINGGROUP.com

SHAW
Copyright © 2022 M. Tasia

ISBN: 978-1-957295-08-4

To my family for their unwavering support.
I love all of you to the moon and back.

SHAW

CHAPTER ONE

Shaw

"So help me god, I will end you," Shaw growled as Rick, Roman's assistant, set a plate down on the counter in front of him.

"You all need to improve your diets," Rick hummed as if he hadn't single-handedly ruined Shaw's meal. "I've replaced your typical breakfast of fat-laden foods packed full of cholesterol with what your bodies truly need."

Shaw looked down at the plate. Where the hell were his fried eggs, sausage, grits, biscuits, and gravy? He looked over at the rest of the confused team before focusing on Roman. "You brought him into this house."

Roman smiled sheepishly but remained silent. When Rick offered to cook breakfast for the team, this shit was the last thing Shaw expected. Now with it in front of him, he chastised himself for not knowing better, considering who'd made the offer.

"And this is for Kyle," Rick said as he added a second plate.

"Hey, why does he get a steak?" Spence huffed. "I want a steak," he complained, sounding like a two-year-old. Who could blame him? Shaw wanted a juicy steak as well.

"Because he's healing and needs extra protein in his diet right now. You other six need to do more clean eating. A fresh organic fruit salad that's never seen the inside of a can, cold-pressed kale and cucumber juice, whole-grain cereal, low-fat milk, and plain yogurt with a touch of wildflower honey."

"I'm going to starve," Fletch moaned as he held a death grip on his fork. "I can't live on this."

"Your body will adapt," Rick stated as if he wasn't destroying breakfast for them. "I've taken the opportunity to fill the cupboards and refrigerator with a variety of clean foods to make it easier for you guys to stay on the program when I'm not here."

Spence jumped up from his chair and stormed over to the snack cupboard, flinging the doors open. Sure enough, the cabinet, which usually contained salty chips, buttery popcorn, sweet candy, and other essential munchies, was now empty. "For fuck's sake. You took my chips. C'mon."

Shaw didn't have the time to argue. He wanted to take Kyle his breakfast. He squinted at Roman. "Fix this," he demanded before turning to head to Kyle's bedroom. He was thankful Rick hadn't messed with Kyle's food. It was hard enough to get him to eat without putting tree bark in front of him. Shaw's stomach growled at the heavenly smell of the meat wafting up temptingly.

Kyle had been healing from severe injuries he sustained to both his legs. The jury was still out on whether he'd ever walk again. He was a good man dealt a crappy hand. Shaw had been by Kyle's side since they found him tied up in a cottage in Seattle. At first, Shaw felt sorry for the guy, but those feelings had morphed, and it worried him.

Fletcher, his SEAL teammate, was Kyle's brother and had been tending him, but for the most part, Shaw had been playing nursemaid and couldn't seem to tear himself away from the compassionate and fierce man. It was driving him nuts. Nothing romantic had ever happened between them, but Shaw was behaving as if Kyle were his responsibility, and at the same time the guy Shaw had been bedding hadn't seen him in months.

Fuck, everything was all screwed up inside his head.

He'd been a loner his entire life and didn't cotton to anything holding him down. Shaw was part of a team, and he cared for each of his SEAL brothers, but that was an entirely different kind of commitment.

When he reached the bedroom, the door was open, but he knocked anyway before walking in. "Breakfast is served," he said cheerfully, which wasn't his style, but Kyle was dealing with depression caused by PTSD from his trauma. Shaw put on the happiness even when he wasn't feeling it. "You're going to like what's on the menu today."

When he'd cleared the doorway, he saw a lump in the center of the queen-size bed buried under a pile of covers with only the tips of Kyle's blond hair showing. The TV was droning on, some nature show, and the drapes were drawn. It was time to open up this place and remind Kyle he was still in the land of the living.

"Trust me when I say you might be the only one enjoying their breakfast this morning," Shaw stated hoping to get a response out of the lump. But no. Nothing.

He set the plates and mugs of coffee on top of the dresser, opened the drapes, and let the sunlight in. Then, he carried a chair over to the side of the bed, grabbed the plates, and brought them closer.

"You don't want your steak getting cold, do you?" He hoped the temptation would be enough to get Kyle up and moving.

Kyle's muffled voice came up through the covers. "Steak?"

"Yep, and it smells delicious. And you got pan-fried potatoes and some fruit." Hell, Shaw was salivating at the description, never mind the aroma. When he looked at his plate, he wanted to hurl.

There was movement from under the blankets. The tuft of blond hair disappeared for a moment before arms appeared through the same opening, and then Kyle slid through, stopping when the covers hit his waist.

"'Morning, man."

"'Morning, Shaw."

"Here you go," he said as he handed Kyle his plate and utensils. "Your coffee is on the side table. Let me know when you want a drink."

"Thanks," Kyle muttered, his blue eyes looking a bit tired. He glanced at Shaw's plate. "What the hell are you eating?"

"A Rick special. We aren't eating right or clean, some shit like that."

Kyle took a long, loving look at Shaw's plate. "I know you two don't get along. Is this some sort of punishment?"

"If it is, you're the only one not being punished. The entire team is being force-fed this shit."

Without hesitation, Kyle lifted his plate and said, "We can share mine."

Shaw couldn't help the warm feeling filling him. Kyle was only four months out of the hospital after surviving brutal beatings that took away his ability to walk. Yet here he was worried about what Shaw was going to eat. He shouldn't be surprised. Kyle was in this condition because he protected innocent women from being sold and trafficked, and for refusing to give in to the shitheads who wanted the evidence he'd gathered against them, and the fucktards who pulled their strings.

"I'm fine," Shaw said before stabbing a piece of honeydew with his fork. "It's not so bad." He did his best not to grimace as he chewed and swallowed. It wasn't that he didn't like melon, but it should be in a bowl next to a plate of fried eggs cooked in butter covered with salt and pepper.

"Okay," Kyle said as he eyed him suspiciously. "If you're sure."

"Positive," Shaw said before taking a spoonful of some funky-looking cereal. He'd be picking twigs out of his teeth for the rest of the day. Maybe he could stop by the diner between errands. A double-stacked bacon cheeseburger with a fried egg was calling his name.

Shaw felt infinitely better when Kyle took his first bite of steak. He needed a lot of energy to heal properly, making each meal more important than usual.

"How'd you sleep last night?" Shaw asked. The first few weeks, he slept in Kyle's room. But when he started healing, and made noises about being babysat, Shaw returned to his bedroom upstairs and slept in his bed. He worried about Kyle, but the bed was a damn sight better than the corner wing chair.

The haunted expression ghosting across Kyle's face made Shaw sorry for asking. "It wasn't too bad. Same old, same old."

Yeah, right. Now wasn't the time to dig into Kyle's nightmares, but Shaw was positive they were brutal. PTSD messed with every part of your body, but the mind was the hardest hit. It could twist and warp memories until you'd be terrified of closing your eyes and could no longer function out in the world.

"Every creak still waking you up?" Kyle nodded. "I know it sucks being wired that way," Shaw said, hoping Kyle would follow his lead, like the countless other times he'd tried to get him to talk it out. This time didn't work either. He wouldn't push. He knew that'd do no good, and Kyle would pull a turtle.

Shaw was no therapist, but he was a former SEAL who'd seen his fair share of fucked-up, and had been close to checking out more times than he cared to count. He could see the trauma of Kyle's memories eating away at him, and they still had the trial to get through since, of course, the bastards responsible wouldn't cop a plea.

Kyle had discovered his and Fletcher's parents were involved in a human trafficking ring running out of Mexico. He'd given them a chance to turn themselves in before he went to the police with his proof. He never got that far. They'd kidnapped their son and tried to force him into revealing the location of the evidence against them.

Talk about fucked up. Your parents wanting you dead. Now his mother was sitting in jail awaiting trial, and many of Seattle's high and mighty were involved. His father was dead, shot while trying to kill Fletcher for saving Kyle. The whole story sounded like a movie, and even Shaw had a hard time believing all of it even though he'd been part of the rescue effort.

"What are your plans today?" Kyle asked, bringing Shaw out of his thoughts.

"I have to run into town for a bit, and then I need to finish scraping the old paint off the east side of the house to get it ready for painting. Spence and I will be heading out next week on a job and I'd like to have it done by then."

"I remember you were saying the client was in California," Kyle muttered as he dug into the fried potatoes.

"Yeah, bodyguard duty for a couple of days while an ambassador is in town. It should be an easy in-and-out job. We don't expect too much fanfare considering it's not an official state visit."

"Why's he going to California?"

"He wants to explore LA like a normal tourist. We're there in case something happens during his travels. A close friend of the ambassador hired us out of what he called an abundance of caution."

Kyle's face darkened, and Shaw tensed. "What's wrong? You in pain?"

"You shouldn't take your safety for granted like that."

No surprise, Kyle had a heightened sensitivity to him putting himself in danger. "I'm not, but compared to other missions, this one isn't teeming with danger. The guy wants to sightsee, that's all."

"Still, something could happen, and if you're not ready, you could be hurt or worse."

"I promise to be careful. Trust me when I say, I've been trained by the best. The Navy SEALs don't fuck around."

Kyle looked like he wanted to say more but stopped himself.

"Hey, bro," Fletcher called as he walked into the room, "we have a date with PT this morning, so eat up. You'll need your energy." Fletcher turned to the closet then asked over his shoulder, "What do you wanna wear?"

Kyle looked at his brother and smiled. "The usual. Sweatpants and a t-shirt. It's not like I'm walking into a boardroom, or even walking at all."

Fletcher's brother was a successful entrepreneur, having sold his first start-up for over thirty million before his life had been turned inside out for trying to do the right thing.

"You will walk again," Fletcher stated firmly. "Get that shit out of your head."

Shaw grabbed his plate and coffee before heading for the door in case he was dragged into another brother-on-brother exchange. The last time he got stuck between the two of them during an argument, both demanded he choose who was right.

"Where are you going?" Fletcher asked.

"Anywhere but here between the two of you. Cheers." Shaw chuckled as he went down the hall and into the kitchen. He'd eaten as much of the "right foods" he could take and wiped off the rest of the sorry excuse of breakfast into the garbage before setting his plate in the new dishwasher. A godsend. It sure beat the hell out of taking turns washing the damn dishes.

Spence was the only person left in the kitchen drinking his coffee.

"Where'd everyone go?" Shaw asked as he looked around.

"My best guess, the diner." Damn, they beat Shaw to it.

"Why didn't you go?"

Spence glanced out the window to where Rick was sitting on the porch typing away on his laptop.

"Oh shit. Him?" Spence smiled and shrugged. "Christ, he'll never leave." Although he was happy for his brother, he couldn't help but think: why couldn't it be someone else? Someone easier to get along with.

Things were getting too complicated around here for Shaw's liking. The guys all partnering up made him antsy.

"Hey, you're going into town. You think you could sneak in a few bags of barbecue chips?" Spence asked with a hopeful grin.

Shaw couldn't help but laugh. "Sure thing, buddy. But eventually he'll," he dipped his head to where Rick was sitting, "catch on to a hidden stash. Then he'll get all riled up again."

A smile burst across Spence's face. "I like it when he gets all flustered."

This right here was why Shaw didn't commit to anyone. Every man he'd ever been with knew the score, and he never hid he was a commitment-phobe. His only real ties were to his team, and that's the way he liked it.

Fletch walked into the kitchen to refill his coffee mug, then turned around and leaned against the counter. "You going to see Bryan today?"

They'd been over this more times than Shaw could count. "Yeah." He and rancher Bryan Murray had an understanding, which didn't involve commitment. They'd been involved since meeting at Clancy's bar weeks before discovering Kyle had been kidnapped.

"Still keeping it loose?"

"C'mon, man. There's nothing more than friendship between Kyle and me, and that's the way it'll stay. I haven't hidden who I am from anyone." Shaw would never lead anyone on. He wasn't one of those heartless bastards.

"If that changes—" Fletch began.

"It won't," Shaw stated firmly.

"Good. Kyle has enough to worry about. He doesn't need to get involved with a committed free agent."

Shaw wouldn't admit Fletch's comment hit home in a way Shaw didn't want to examine. But he was who he was. He'd grown up without any solid, steady people in his life, and he'd learned how to protect himself. After going it alone for so long, he found he was better off fending for himself.

There was no way in hell he'd change after all these years.

CHAPTER TWO

Kyle

Kyle watched as the oak and juniper trees whizzed by his passenger window. He'd had plenty of time to read up on the area where he was now residing: Texas Hill Country. It was truly beautiful and entirely different from what he'd been used to living in Seattle, where it rained about half the year. Here there were magnificent blue skies for miles, and pillowy clouds usually filled those skies. It lightened his mood until he remembered where they were headed.

He wasn't looking forward to PT, especially knowing he'd be wiped out for the rest of the day afterward. But it was a necessary evil if he ever wanted to walk again. Dear old dad did a number on his legs, trying to get him to reveal the location of the evidence he'd gathered against the asshole and his colleagues. Kyle would be damned if he'd allow his insane father win.

However, most of the time, his legs struggled to cooperate with his plans. Giving up wasn't an option, and it would never be. No matter how messed up his head was, Kyle refused to relent on his physical recovery. His parents' evil actions wouldn't define the remainder of his life.

"Will we have a chance to stop and check in on Alejandra and the others today?" Kyle asked.

Alejandra was the woman he'd found hiding behind his parents' garage all those many months ago. She was the catalyst for everything that happened after he'd met her. The whole human trafficking scheme of taking young women from Mexico to work as servants for the rich and powerful of Seattle had crumbled after their clandestine meeting.

"How about we wait and see how you feel after PT?" Fletcher, his older brother, suggested.

He had a point. "Guess you're right." Though he was loath to admit it.

Fletcher and his friends, a retired SEALs team, had saved him from what assuredly would've been his death. There was no doubt in his mind his parents intended to get rid of him once they had what they wanted. Sick but true.

He and his brother had always had a special bond, no matter how estranged Fletcher was from the rest of the family. Kyle remembered multiple occasions when his father had sat him down when the old man was a garden-variety bastard who thought the sun shone out his ass—before he turned into a crazed lunatic—and demanded Kyle cut ties with his older brother. He never knew why they behaved so horribly toward Fletcher, but Kyle rejected all attempts at forcing him to do the same.

His brother was a good and honorable man who risked his life to protect others and their freedoms. Hell, Fletcher had almost died shutting down a factory providing bombs to militants in some desert while Kyle sat safely at home. That deserved respect, not the shit his parents doled out.

"Um, bro, can we talk?" Fletcher asked, sounding a bit nervous.

"I'm all ears."

"What's going on between you and Shaw?"

Kyle wasn't surprised they'd rounded back to this question again. His brother was protective, to say the least, and persistent.

"We're friends."

"You remember me telling you he's a…"

"'Manslut' was the word you used."

The corner of Fletcher's lips turned up into a sly grin he always wore. "Well, yeah. Don't get me wrong. Shaw is a stand-up guy. A friend, and a good man to have at your back, but when it comes to the men he's dated, he's a commitment-phobe."

"I've been told this a time or two before," Kyle said, wondering when it would stop, and why Fletcher kept pestering him. Shaw had been kind and generous with his time, but nothing more. He'd been the ballast Kyle needed when he was at his worst.

"I don't want you to get any ideas in your head," Fletcher warned.

Kyle let out an exasperated breath. "You do realize I'm an adult in my thirties in complete control of my mental faculties?"

"Yeah. But you're injured and vulnerable."

"Vulnerable?" Kyle saw red, and he turned toward his brother. "I have never been vulnerable in my life. Even when I was tied up in that room, I refused to be another of their victims and kept the location of the evidence safe no matter what they did. Vulnerable is not a word I would use to describe myself ever, and I never want to hear it again."

Fletcher's face flushed. "I'm sorry. I know how strong you are. You're stronger than most trained men I know."

"Then trust me to know what's best for me."

"You know where he's off to today?"

"Yeah," Kyle answered. "To run errands and no doubt visit his current 'boyfriend' Bryan, who's a rancher somewhere around here. Shaw told me they met at the bar in town, and Bryan sounds like a good guy."

Fletcher slowed the truck and looked over at Kyle. "He's told you everything?"

"Of course he has. We're friends. He's helped me through some pretty rough shit when all I wanted to do was disappear. His presence is calming and reassuring. Don't misunderstand me. Shaw is one hell of a gorgeous man, but I know the score. My eyes are wide open, bro."

"I think I owe Shaw an apology," Fletcher mumbled.

"You probably do," Kyle agreed as they pulled into the medical center. He could imagine the hell his brother was giving Shaw. "But I love you for caring about me and my 'widdle' heart," he teased his protective big brother.

Fletch's laughter filled the cab of the truck as he'd hoped. "Okay, okay. I get it," he said while holding his hands up in surrender.

"Good," Kyle said. "I've got enough to worry about than who's fucking who. Or is it whom? I never remember."

Fletch gave him a look that said, *Has anyone ever mistaken me for an English teacher?* He shook his head. "Speaking of, have you even been on a date with a man?" Fletcher asked, and Kyle understood his curiosity, considering he'd only recently jumped out of the closet. He felt bad for not sharing his news with his brother earlier, but fear was a powerful motivator in their family.

"Hell, I haven't even had the opportunity to make it to first base with one. I couldn't risk it living in the same city as our parents. I know it was cowardly." He wasn't proud of his behavior, but he did what he had to do to survive.

"Hold it right there. You're no coward. I understand the pressure you were under, and we both know what would've happened if they'd found out," Fletcher near growled. Kyle knew his brother had detested their parents before all this shit went down. Now? He'd said on more than one occasion he wished he could resurrect their father so he could kill him again, and torture wasn't off the table.

"It's something I need to work through," Kyle explained. "Over time."

Fletcher nodded as he pulled into a parking spot and turned off the engine. "How you feeling about PT now that you've been at it for over a month?"

"Truthfully, at first, I didn't see the use. I thought the damage to my legs was too extensive, but I was willing to try. Now I think Dr. Thomas might be the best bet for me walking again."

His brother's face lit up. "That's wonderful news."

Kyle couldn't help the hopeful smile that broke out and hurt his cheeks. He hadn't smiled a lot lately and was out of practice. His mind was filled with what-ifs and doubts, but he had to try to push those aside.

He could do this.

CHAPTER THREE

Shaw

The diner wasn't busy when Shaw walked in, setting off the chimes hanging above the front door. Most of the breakfast crew were long gone by now. He'd seen Brick and Roman as they were leaving with smiles on their faces. Proving eating tree bark for breakfast did not make a normal man happy. Steak and eggs did.

The neon signs flashed in the windows as the sun rose higher into the sky and gleamed off the stainless-steel exterior. He didn't bother sitting at a booth. Instead, he took a seat on a barstool in front of the long Formica counter. There was no need to take out the well-worn menu since he knew what he wanted. He'd been dreaming about it since hopping in his truck.

"What can I get you, honey?" the waitress asked. Donna looked to be in her eighties and still going strong.

"Double bacon cheeseburger, fries, water, and a coffee, please." His usual.

"You got it, dear. Be back with your coffee and water in a second," she said as she walked over to the kitchen window and called out his order to the cook before attaching the paper to a metal carousel.

"Thanks, Donna."

Shaw looked out the large bank of windows at the small town of Marshall. Clancy's bar was across the street, and the grocery store was farther down the road. There were a lot of dirt roads in this area, but the town center was paved. A bank stood on the corner, which was attached to the post office and library. The public elementary, middle, and high schools were down the first side street past the diner.

There were stores with decorated windows displaying their wares, a barber shop, a salon, and a gas station. Across town were a medical clinic and a trauma center. Shaw had to admit it wasn't a bad place to live. It had all the necessities, and he could easily drive to bigger cities within an hour or so if necessary. He'd never lived in a place this rural and was surprised by how much he liked it.

"Here you go, dear," Donna said as she set down his water and coffee.

"Thanks, ma'am."

Shaw added the cream and sugar before taking a long drink of the hot beverage. Perfect. He grabbed a newspaper from the end of the counter and began reading through the local news. There was an auction this Saturday over at the stockyards outside of town, the local knitting bee was looking for new members, and there was going to be a bake sale at the high school to raise money for new football uniforms.

"Yep, another day in paradise," he chuckled and set the paper down.

"Well, I don't know about paradise," Donna said as she set the beefy burger down in front of him. "But it's mighty nice."

"That it is. How's the husband doing today?"

"As ornery as ever. The man needs to relax."

"What's got him fired up now?"

"The neighbor's new dog, if that's what you want to call it. The thing's the size of a small cat," she explained. "It's decided hubby's newly planted garden is the perfect place to do its business."

"What's he going to do about the dog?"

"He was setting out traps when I left for work this morning."

"Traps." Shaw coughed as he tried to swallow a mouth full of coffee before he sprayed it all over the counter. "You're going to trap the neighbor's dog?"

"They're humane traps. Geez, we don't want to kill it. Only scare it away from the gardens." Donna looked at him like his head wasn't screwed on tight.

"Thank god. I was picturing him setting up snares all over your yard and catching all the neighborhood's pets."

Donna began laughing. "Maybe that would get our neighbor's attention. So far, they don't seem to care where the bitty thing does its business. You know, I think if it were a real full-size dog, hubby would respect it more than the yappy footlong slipper dog."

Shaw couldn't help but laugh. Some people couldn't stand the chihuahuas of this world, either in dog or human form. He could respect that.

After she left to take another customer's order, Shaw tucked into his burger with gusto. The bacon, cheese, and beef exploded in his mouth with flavor, further distinguishing itself from Rick's idea of food. Juicy ten-ounce patties of beef blended with the crispy, salty bacon helped wipe away all memory of the grazing he was forced to do this morning.

He didn't stop eating until the burger was gone, then, with the same gusto, he followed with the fries and the glass of water. Relaxing back, he drank the last few sips of his coffee before pulling out his wallet and leaving enough money for lunch and a tip. Donna was taking another customer's order at a booth, so he tucked the money under his plate to be safe. He'd seen the worst of human behavior, and trust was earned.

Now he was ready for what he hoped the afternoon would bring.

***

Shaw's heart raced as he drove down the long, dusty laneway and up to the large ranch on the hill. An expansive single-story house spread out before him, and farther back, a trio of red barns stood guard in the noon sun. Various corrals held either horses or Texas longhorn cattle, and Shaw could see a couple of ranch hands working in the distance.

He pulled his truck to a stop beside the large back deck and sat staring at the house for several minutes. What was he doing sitting here filled with yearning? He was imagining what it would be like living on this ranch. He threw open the driver's door with more force than necessary and got out before slamming it shut. It was bad enough he couldn't get Bryan out of his mind. Now he was pining like some lovesick teenager.

"Whiskey, tango, foxtrot. Who pissed in your cornflakes?" A familiar voice laughed from the other side of his truck.

Shaw came around the back of his truck and found Bryan's grandfather sitting in his usual spot inside one of the three bays of the attached garage. He had that one bay tricked out into the man cave of Shaw's dreams. Pool table, old-school video arcade games, full bar, and a jukebox covered in neon. A ramp led up to an internal door that opened into the kitchen, making it easier for Isaiah to navigate his electric wheelchair in and out of the house.

"Afternoon, Mr. Murray."

"Good afternoon, Shaw. You seem a bit high-strung today, son."

Shaw raked his hand down his face before answering. "Got a lot on my mind right now, is all. Sorry, sir."

"No worries. If you're here to visit with Bryan, I'm sorry to say it was a wasted trip. He's out checking the fence lines, and he never returns before nightfall."

Shaw's mood sank even further. He'd texted Bryan that he'd be coming by, which explained why he hadn't received a reply. Either he was out of cell range, was too busy to check his phone, or he'd decided to stop waiting for Shaw to get his ass out to the ranch.

Their agreement to keep everything light and without expectations or commitment didn't work for everyone, and perhaps Bryan had come to that realization. After the initial exploration and sex, some had a change of heart and wanted more, but that was one thing he could never give.

"Would you please let him know I stopped by?" He could hear the defeat in his voice and hated it. What the hell was wrong with him recently?

"Well, I'll be damned." Isaiah laughed while pointing past the last barn on the left.

Sure enough, a lone trail of dust being kicked up by a horse's hooves was heading their way. Bryan was riding full out, his black hair flying in the wind as he held his Stetson in his hand. His strong arm and legs held him in place atop his powerful mustang, Ranger, as they crossed the pasture leading from what Bryan had called his back forty, a rocky area containing the natural spring that fed many of the ranches in this area, and was counted on for drinking water.

Shaw tried to stamp down the excitement building in his gut, but it was no use. The closer the cowboy got, the faster Shaw's heart raced, and the more fine-tuned his hearing and sight became, as if he were on a mission deep in enemy territory. The horse slowed as Bryan slid off the side of his saddle, his feet hitting the ground before the muscular mustang stopped.

Releasing the reins, Bryan kept walking until he stood directly in front of Shaw. The scent of leather and sweat from hard work filled Shaw's senses as Bryan's piercing blue eyes looked him up and down and then he licked his lips as if Shaw were a tall glass of ice water.

If that wasn't an invitation, he didn't know what was, and he knew a thing or two about the matter. He might be commitment adverse, but he was a hell of a flirt.

Before he knew what was happening, Isaiah, who was laughing his ass off, had Ranger's reins, and the animal seemed perfectly content to follow the electric wheelchair toward the barn. Shaw couldn't take his eyes off the gorgeous man in front of him, Stetson in hand, covered in dust and sweat. Nothing had ever looked better.

They were the same height with roughly the same build, but where Bryan was dark, Shaw was light. Bryan's darker features and short black hair contrasted with Shaw's tanned but paler skin, and long blond hair. Like night and day.

"'Bout time you turned up." Bryan's deep voice resonated throughout Shaw's body, making certain parts perk right up.

"Didn't know I was on the clock."

Bryan lifted his rough, calloused hand and gently tucked a stray hair behind Shaw's right ear. "We'll have to get you a new clock." His sexy-as-sin Southern drawl had Shaw entranced.

Damn, he was in deep.

***

Bryan

Bryan ran the tips of his fingers through Shaw's silky hair. He doubted he'd ever seen a purer golden color in his life. His lover's pale blue eyes watched his every move as he wrapped his hand around the back of Shaw's neck and pulled him in for a long-needed kiss. It'd been a while since the handsome man had come around, and no one could blame Bryan for assuming their time together was over.

He knew the score: no commitment, and he'd agreed to it. Nothing more needed to be said, except for the utter relief and excitement he'd felt when he received Shaw's text letting him know he was on the way. Stupid, but unavoidable, Bryan had gone ahead and become attached to the unattachable. He intended to keep that his little secret.

The feel of Shaw's soft lips against his own brought out a possessive need to leave Bryan's mark on his lover. He pulled him closer and took command of the kiss. His tongue explored every inch of Shaw's mouth while his hands did the same with his body. His

Stetson dropped onto a nearby chair, allowing him to explore this delicious man while reacquainting himself with every hill and valley created by Shaw's muscled arms and chest.

By the sounds coming from him, he was right there with Bryan: desperate to get closer. Before he began stripping the man out of his clothing right there in front of the garage, Bryan pulled away, grabbed onto Shaw's hand, and led him through the man cave and up into the house.

Bryan didn't bother slowing down and headed for his bedroom suite at the other end of the long hallway traversing the ranch house. They'd have all the privacy in the world back there, and his grandfather would make sure they weren't disturbed. Shaw didn't hesitate as he matched him step for step, giving Bryan the impression Shaw would be leading if they were at his house.

There was something crazy about the raw need they shared every time they were near one another. He'd felt it the day they met at Clancy's Bar all those many months ago, and it had been growing in intensity ever since.

They didn't slow their pace until they walked into his bedroom and the door slammed shut behind them. The room wasn't much. A king-size bed and a couple of dressers served him well enough.

"I need to have a shower," Bryan said as he began stripping out of his dirt-stained button-up.

Shaw bent over, took off his boots, and didn't bother looking up when he answered. "I'll wash your back."

"Hell yeah," Bryan almost cheered. "That's an offer I'll happily accept."

With increased speed, he tore off his boots and jeans until he was left standing in his black boxer briefs. Before he turned to the bathroom, he needed one more kiss and took the opportunity to wrap his arms around Shaw's broad shoulders and hairless chest before diving in for his lover's lips once again. Bryan was a bear with his thick, dark chest hair compared to Shaw.

Shaw's moans were spurring him on, but Bryan managed to pull himself away using a considerable amount of restraint. "If we keep this up, we'll never make it to the shower," he said as he gasped for air, "and I need to wash all this dust off."

"Agreed."

Bryan turned and headed for the bathroom, assured Shaw would follow. When he reached his walk-in shower, he turned on the water and was about to turn around when Shaw wrapped him in his arms from behind. The feel of those strong arms and hot flesh was intoxicating, and Bryan needed more.

Reaching back, he cupped Shaw's balls through his cotton boxer briefs and slid the fingers of his other hand around his thick cock. Shaw's deep growl and moans urged Bryan on. It was the sweetest music he'd ever heard.

Shaw's hands began to wander as well. First, he stopped at Bryan's sensitive nipples as he rolled them between his thumb and index finger until they ached before pinching them and sending Bryan to the moon. His back arched, and a low groan was ripped from his chest from the pleasure/pain pulling and rubbing.

Steam began drifting from the shower and wound around them in a caress of warmth. Shaw's hands traveled farther down Bryan's body until he deftly tucked his fingers under the waistband of his boxer briefs and slid them to his ankles. By the time he kicked off the scant fabric and turned to face Shaw, the man was already naked and looking at him like he was a prime Grade A steak fresh off the grill.

Bryan couldn't help the smile that broke over his face. He'd never been happier than when Shaw was around. Another aspect of this relationship he'd have to monitor so it didn't get out of hand because when all was said and done, Shaw would be leaving sooner or later.

"Hey, what's wrong?" Shaw asked as he took Bryan into his arms. "Your smile faded."

Yep, he'd need to be much more careful. "I was thinking about the tracks I found out in the back forty." It wasn't a lie. He had found horse and boot tracks in the dried mud from the rains that'd hit Marshall last week. But that wasn't the real reason his expression had changed.

"Is anyone supposed to be out there?" Shaw asked while tracing Bryan's jawline with his thumb.

"No. It's private property. Part of our ranch lands," Bryan said, but quickly veered off into a more pleasurable direction. "But let's forget I mentioned it." He grinned. "We have better things to do." He wanted to get back to what he'd been doing with his Navy SEAL.

"I'm confident I can take your mind off everything," Shaw promised while leading him into the shower. Something about Shaw's expression told Bryan this conversation wasn't over.

The hot water felt good against his aching muscles. Ranch life was hard, especially when he had hundreds of head of fifteen-hundred-pound cattle sporting sharp horns that grew up to one hundred inches tip to tip. Texas Longhorn cattle weren't to be messed with.

Bryan groaned as Shaw positioned him directly under the stream of hot water and began massaging his tight shoulders. It felt luxurious having someone taking care of him for a change, and he leaned into it.

"That's it," Shaw murmured as he concentrated on Bryan's right shoulder, which Shaw knew had been dislocated a couple of times over the years, mainly from when Bryan had competed in rodeos.

"Feels so good," he moaned. "Thank you, babe."

Babe? Shit. Bryan had never used endearments with Shaw. It felt too personal considering their arrangement, which was weird to say given they'd had sex, a most personal. This was messing with his head.

Instead of looking for an escape hatch, Shaw smiled and continued massaging Bryan's shoulder. He'd been under the impression any sign of attachment would send his lover running. *Hmm.*

He began exploring Shaw's wet body, wanting to memorize as much as he could. Bryan raked his short fingernails across his lover's chest and nipples, eliciting Shaw's appreciative groan.

Pulling the handsome man even closer, he reclaimed those soft lips in a heated kiss, all tongues and teeth. Need drove him forward until their hot, wet bodies pressed firmly together under the soothing stream of water in a hedonistic display that drove Bryan to the brink of coming. He reached down and took hold of Shaw's thick cock, breaking their kiss.

"If you keep that up," Shaw growled, "you're gonna make me come."

"One's all you got in you, frog man?" Bryan crooned while licking a bead of water from Shaw's neck.

"Challenge accepted," Shaw stated with a devilish smile.

"Bring it on," Bryan said as he began pumping Shaw's thick cock. "Show me whatcha got."

Shaw's eyes lit up, and his laser-like gaze fixed on Bryan like a predator looking for his supper. It was one hell of a heady feeling being the center of Shaw's piercing attention. The intensity was unmatched.

"You'd better hang on, cowboy. This ride ain't no eight seconds."

Bryan chuckled at the bull riding reference. Shaw was one of a kind, and the man was all his. At least for the moment.

Shaw reached around and cupped Bryan's right butt cheek while his other hand took hold of his throbbing cock. He couldn't stop the moan that was ripped from his throat at his lover's touch. Both men shook with every thrust, kiss, and bite. The hot steam surrounded them, blanketing their bodies in a veil of privacy where only the two of them existed.

After several minutes, Shaw groaned, "Fuck, Bryan." His head was thrown back as his cock pulsed in Bryan's hand. Streams of warmth splashed against their abs, adding another layer to the sensory experience before Shaw moved his index finger and began circling Bryan's hole.

Starbursts went off in his head, clouding his vision the moment Shaw slid his finger in deep. Bryan's world exploded as fire raced down his spine, into his balls, and out the end of his cock in one long, hard orgasm.

He was sure he was going to pass out at any moment, but Shaw held him tight as they both fought to breathe. The intimacy they shared was real, no matter how fleeting their time together might be.

Shaw tightened his hold for a few seconds before saying, "Let's get you washed up, and then we can see about doing that again, but horizontally in bed."

"Damn right," Bryan agreed as Shaw reached for the bar of soap.

"Stand still so I can lather you up."

"Seriously, you think I can be still when your hands are rubbing all over me? I have no self-restraint when you're involved." Shaw flashed a wicked grin before going to work on Bryan's arms followed by his chest and abdomen. It seemed as if the tough-as-nails SEAL had a tender side under all those layers of gruff and bravado.

Bryan closed his eyes and sunk into the feeling of the soapy sponge running over his body in soothing circles. Ironic how the same gentle hands that were soothing away his aches and pains could also be lethal weapons.

"Turn around."

Bryan complied and he braced his hands against the warm shower tiles before hanging his head under the stream of hot water. His groans turned to moans of pleasure as sore muscles were soothed and tight knots unraveled. The man had magic in those hands, and he was one fortunate cowboy.

Just as he was getting ready to melt down the drain the sharp sting of an open palmed slap across his ass cheeks was followed by a deep chuckle. "That might leave a mark but having my handprint on your ass doesn't sound all that bad to me." Shaw laughed before turning to the shower door.

Bryan couldn't help himself, he slapped his palm across Shaw's toned ass cheeks, making him holler. "You're right, it does have a certain appeal," he said at Shaw's shocked look. Bryan took the opportunity to bolt past his lover, grab a towel, and race out into his bedroom and to the other side of his king-size bed.

Shaw wasn't far behind, his smirk in place. "If you wanted me to redden your ass, all you had to do was ask," he said from the other side of the room, probably calculating how quickly he could launch himself over the bed.

"Turnabout is fair play." Bryan knew the big guy could probably cross the bed in a couple strides, but he couldn't help taunting him.

"Oh, I know who's going to be turned about once I get my hands on you."

Bryan couldn't stop his laughter and took off the second Shaw made his move. It felt great hearing the usually serious man let loose and have fun. Bryan tried to include laughter every time they were together. It made his heart thud hearing those deep chuckles and outright laughter fill the room.

He rounded the headboard when he felt Shaw's arm wrap around his waist and suddenly, he was airborne and heading for the mattress. The moment he landed on the plush comforter his body was blanketed by the weight of his lover. Nothing had ever felt so good.

"You're in for it now," Shaw growled into his ear, sending flames of desire down his spine. Whatever "it" was, he wanted it with every fiber of his being.

Bent fingers came ominously close to his ribs before they struck. "C'mon, man. You know how ticklish I am." But his cries fell on deaf ears as Shaw went to work, fully engaged in tormenting him.

It wasn't long before he cried "Uncle" in the middle of the bed with Shaw straddling him. His smile was electric, and in a move straight out of some action movie, he captured Bryan's hands and pinned them above his head. Shaw's focus was on Bryan completely as he used his free hand to run his blunt fingernails across his chest. When they scraped over his nipples, Bryan almost shot off the bed.

The move had to've been intentional since Shaw knew how much Bryan liked nipple play. The growl that followed, along with the gleam in his lover's eyes, promised they were far from over.

"Have you learned your lesson?" Shaw asked after successfully subduing him.

I've always had a problem with lessons." Bryan chuckled. "We might have to do this over again until I get it right. Do you mind bending over?"

This time his growl was quickly followed up by a take-no-prisoners kiss that rocked Bryan down to his toes. Damn. The man knew how to kiss.

Their tongues explored as their naked bodies pressed together. He wasn't sure when his hands had been released, but as soon as he realized he was free he went about mapping the tanned and toned body on top of him.

It wasn't long before they were both moaning and he felt the bed shift. Bryan didn't stop his exploration when the side table draw was pulled open and items were dropped onto the bed.

He licked his way up Shaw's thick neck, stopping to nibble along the way. They were as close as two people could be, but he still needed more.

"Stick that gorgeous cock inside me."

"That's what I intend to do," Shaw answered while lubing up his fingers.

All thought left his mind when Shaw's fingers circled his hole. Pinpricks of light flashed through his vision as the first finger slid in deep. "That's it. Yes, right there," Bryan babbled as the finger brushed against his prostate and the pinprick's became fireworks. "More. I need more."

A second finger joined the first and stretched his hole to accommodate Shaw's large cock. By the time a third and final finger sunk deep Bryan was panting and moaning uncontrollably. He watched as Shaw opened the condom wrapper and rolled the latex down his shaft. Bryan couldn't help reaching up to give his lover's cock a few pumps.

Shaw's hiss and groan made Bryan's cock pulse with need.

"Ready?"

"Damn right I am."

Shaw smiled wide as he lined up his cock with Bryan's hole and showcased his control by slowly sliding deep. When Shaw bottomed out, Bryan took a few moments to allow his body to relax and grow accustomed to the stretch.

"Take all the time you need," Shaw said as he nibbled on Bryan's ear. "I'll only move when you're comfortable."

Bryan sucked in a deep breath and adjusted his hips until he found the right position and he was ready. His body yearned to be fucked by this man and he didn't want to wait one more second. He reached up and squeezed Shaw's neck, giving him the go-ahead.

Shaw reared up, took hold of both Bryan's knees, raising his lower half up off the mattress before pulling out and slowly pushing back in.

"I'm good, let those hips fly."

"Thank god. Hmmm. You feel so good."

Before Bryan could even think to respond, Shaw pulled out a second time and thrusted forward, shaking the entire bed.

"Yesss." Whatever thought came after that was obliterated by the crushing pace his lover set. His legs went into the air until he was bent like a taco. He felt Shaw adjust his hips and Bryan's world exploded with color and sensations as his prostate was pegged with every thrust. His orgasm raced through him for a second time that day, splashing across his abdomen as his hole clamped down on Shaw's cock.

"Fuck, yeah," Shaw shouted while pushing himself in deep, and his cries were followed by a deep, guttural growl as he came, filling the latex. "Shit, you're going to be the death of me."

"Same."

Bryan lowered his legs as Shaw tied off the condom and threw it in the trash before diving into bed and pulling Bryan close.

"So, you give up then," Shaw stated.

"Not a chance."

Shaw chuckled, making Bryan wonder what Shaw had in mind. When he reached for the side table drawer, Bryan had his answer. *Yesss.*

Later that day, after Shaw had annihilated the challenge and the two of them lay entwined in bed, Bryan couldn't help but fall deeper under the SEAL's spell. All the warning signs in the world meant nothing as he raced on to his destruction. His eyes were wide open and there'd be no one to blame but himself when it ended and he was left wanting.

Shaw ran the palm of his big hand across Bryan's back, leaving a trail of goosebumps in his wake. To hell with reason and common sense. He'd worked hard keeping this ranch alive after both of his parents' deaths. When they needed extra money to pay the ranch hands or feed his cattle, Bryan would enter rodeos across Texas and other western states. It was a brutal sport and he was successful doing it.

He rode bulls. The meaner the better, and frequently, the bulls took their due. More than once Bryan found himself paying with bruised or broken bones for weeks or even months. Hell, he owned a cane especially for that reason, and the night he and Shaw met he was nursing a hurt knee from a rodeo in San Antonio. But it was worth it to keep the Double M Ranch afloat and his parents' legacies intact.

Now, he deserved something unpredictable and dangerous that had to do with his heart instead of his body.

And Shaw fit the bill to a T.

Bryan knew the rules, and understood he was taking the kind of chance that could crush him.

But the heart wants what the heart wants.

Logic be damned.

CHAPTER FOUR

Shaw

Shaw parked his truck where he usually did, alongside Fletcher's, and jumped out. He'd been gone most of the day and had thoroughly enjoyed every second. So much for scraping the old paint off the house, but he refused to feel guilty. It'd been weeks since he'd had a chance to see Bryan, and he wasn't going to rush their time together when he had the opportunity to spend time with his cowboy.

The whole thing was totally out of character for him. He was never in a rush to make it back to any lover. More often than not, he would've already found a replacement. It sounded callous, and maybe it was, but it was his way of surviving.

He learned early on in his childhood people weren't meant to be faithful. He'd grown up in a community of polyamorous couples, which in and of itself wasn't a bad thing, but a kid shouldn't've known about it. Unfortunately, his parents were the poster children for the lifestyle, and weren't discreet. They didn't shield Shaw from their relationships, and never explained why their front door revolved like the entrance to a large hotel. Imagine how he felt growing up and seeing men and women going into, and often sleeping in, his parents' bedroom with one or both of them.

He'd learned from an early age commitment was a farce, along with marital vows. Useless words meant to bind lovers together for life, weren't worth the paper they'd been written on. In his parents' case, twenty-four hours after the wedding they'd invited others into their bed. Or so he'd been told.

In truth, he couldn't be sure the man who was married to his mother was his biological father. He didn't know if it was one of the other men from their circle, and it didn't seem to matter to his parents. It messed with him not knowing if his dad was his real father or if it was Mr. Carter, who lived down the street.

With a growl and sharp shake of his head, he pushed down the memories and carried on into the lake house to find Julia, Brick, and Roman sitting around the kitchen table looking through stacks of paper; some pieces were crumpled and others stained by age and, he guessed, the leaky roof.

"Hey, whatcha guys doing?" he asked as he neared the table.

"Julia found all of this stuffed into a banker's box in the back of Sophia's closet," Roman answered. "Isn't it fantastic?"

Brick had slowly been clearing out and donating his Great-Aunt Sophia's belongings. He'd kept a few mementos along the way, saying Sophia would've laughed at how he was behaving, and would've told him to donate it all and be done with it. Shaw had never met Sophia, but he sure wished he had. She sounded like a no-nonsense woman who cared deeply for the people she loved.

"What is it?" Other than old, musty paper. Most of the documents didn't look salvageable.

"A journal. Maybe a family history," Julia said. "There are even references to people and places in Marshall."

"All the paper has been worn and faded to some degree. It's hard to put it all together," Roman added as he picked up a random piece of paper, flattened it, and added it to the pile to his right. "And none of it is in order," he huffed as he sat back in his chair. "How was your visit over at Double M Ranch?"

"All right." That was his business, and he wasn't the type to share.

"I miss the days you'd return from leave with all these stories about the men you bedded," Brick said with a grin. "But," he shrugged, "I respect your privacy."

"Thanks, man."

"You don't need to hear about his exploits when you have me," Roman said while tossing a few crumpled pieces of paper at Brick.

"This is so exciting," Julia cheered. "I can't wait to piece this together."

"Well, I guess you've got a mystery on your hands," Shaw said before turning toward Kyle's bedroom. "Is Kyle awake? How did PT go?"

"He looked beat when Fletch brought him home, and Kyle hasn't come out of his room since," Julia said while still digging into a cardboard box. "I brought him a late lunch earlier, but he's been quiet."

"I'll go see how he's doing," Shaw said, turning around and walking away before anyone could say a word or sucker him into helping dig through those old pages.

He could hear what sounded like semiautomatic gunfire the closer he got to Kyle's door. He knocked and waited for him to answer. When he did, Shaw walked in to find Kyle playing one of the new games on the Game Station he'd bought to help Kyle pass the time while he was stuck in bed.

"How was PT?" Shaw asked before sitting on his usual chair beside the bed.

"Same ol', same ol'," he grumbled. "Stretch this, lift that, push, push, push. Hell, you'd think I was in labor or some shit."

Not good. Time for a change of subject. "How's the game?"

"I'm kicking butt and taking names," Kyle said with his first genuine smile since Shaw had walked in.

"This I've gotta see." Shaw laughed and turned to look at the screen.

"I can do you one better," Kyle said as he threw the second game controller to him. "Why don't you join in?"

"I wouldn't want to ruin your winning streak by taking you out," Shaw answered, egging on Kyle.

"You think so. I think you're afraid to take me on."

"I'm not afraid of anything." Shaw puffed out his chest and flexed his arms.

"That's a lie. Everyone has something that they're frightened of." Kyle laughed. "But keep telling yourself that."

Shaw knew exactly what frightened him, but instead of answering, he grabbed the second controller off the bed and said, "Remember, I warned you."

Kyle's laugh got louder, making Shaw smile before getting himself under control. "We'll see about that."

Shaw already had a character created in the game from when he and Kyle had played before, so he chose that player and joined the game. He understood Kyle didn't want to rehash PT or really anything to do with his recovery.

Understandably, all he wanted was to lose himself in a game.

Shaw could help him with that.

***

Kyle

"Hey, no fair. The Navy trained you," Kyle argued as his avatar went down in a hail of bullets.

"Warned you," Shaw snickered from beside him.

Kyle's character respawned in a different location. "We'll just see about that."

On it went, back and forth. One time Kyle would be faster and more accurate, the next, it was Shaw. Kyle couldn't help but wonder if the highly trained SEAL was allowing him to win, but he'd take it as a win after the day he'd had.

His therapist's gung-ho attitude had changed for the first time today. Instead of strictly training him to walk again, they were slipping in strength training for his arms. His only conclusion was to prepare him to be using his arms to push his wheelchair for long periods. They'd even thrown in navigating around obstacles saying it was only to make his life easier for now, but why hadn't that been important before today?

God, he had to get out of his head.

"How was your visit with Bryan?" He needed to think of something else.

The game paused. *Damn.*

"We had a good visit, and that reminds me, Bryan has offered to have you out to take a ride on one of his horses," Shaw said with a smile as if this were some great gift.

"Ride a horse? Seriously?" Kyle said as he waved his hand over his useless legs. "I don't think that's a good idea. I'll have to pass."

"Lots of people in wheelchairs ride horses. They even have Equestrian as a sport in the Paralympics." Shaw's head turned to the side like it always did when trying to understand something.

"This chair isn't permanent," Kyle responded, perhaps a bit sharper than he'd intended. His emotions were all over the place.

"I never said it was," Shaw stated while looking confused.

"Then why'd you mention the Paralympics?"

"As an example of how common it is for people with disabilities to ride a horse. They even use horses for therapy."

Kyle knew Shaw was being logical and calm, but that didn't matter. "I'm not disabled. This is a blip on the radar. I'll get back on my feet," he said dismissively, hoping to end the conversation.

"And getting out of the house for anything other than PT might do you some good." There Shaw went being all logical and annoying.

"I'm fine right where I am, thank you."

"Why are you being so defensive?"

"I'm not being defensive," Kyle yelled, shocking even himself. Maybe he was a bit high-strung, but who could blame him after such a dismal display at PT that morning?

Hell, when they finally worked on his legs, he couldn't get them to respond the way they used to, or at all. Everything was messed up, and his legs' nerves were sending incorrect messages to his muscles. All culminating with him stuck in the damn chair more often than not. His frustration was beginning to show through the cracks of his usually levelheaded self.

Shaw raised his right eyebrow but said nothing. Yep, he was being defensive and a jerk.

"I'm sorry."

"Accepted. Now, what's going on?" Shaw asked with nothing but concern on his face. No anger or annoyance to be seen. Making him feel all the more like an asshole.

"A bad day, I guess," Kyle mumbled, not ready to share his suspicions PT was preparing him for a lifetime in a wheelchair.

"Let's get one thing straight between you and me. If you're unwilling to share it, don't make things up. Just tell me straight you don't wanna talk about it. Okay?"

Kyle let out a deep breath he hadn't realized he'd been holding. "Okay. I'm not ready to talk about it."

With a nod, Shaw restarted the game, and the two of them lost themselves in the secret hideout underneath a mountain range, no longer adversaries but on the same team, and hell yeah, they were kicking butt.

His bedroom filled with hollered instructions, whoops, and laughter.

At least the day was ending on a high note, as it always seemed to with Shaw around.

CHAPTER FIVE

Bryan

Bryan rode Ranger to the outer edges of the ranch property in an attempt to clear his head, but when he reached the last fence post, he wasn't any closer to an answer. It'd been a couple of days since he'd seen Shaw, and he was working hard at keeping his perspective.

He knew his time with the handsome SEAL had an expiration date, but was having a hard time accepting that reality. The emotions he felt coming from Shaw were not from a man who didn't want to feel loved.

Was Shaw intentionally avoiding these emotions, or was he in denial? Although Bryan suspected denial, he didn't know on which side of the fence his lover fell. He couldn't help but wonder what had happened in Shaw's life to make him so skeptical of commitment.

Ranger began kicking up a fuss, and before he knew it, Bryan was on his ass on the hard ground. The telltale rattle made him freeze to the spot when he tried to stand. A Western diamondback made its presence known, and anyone who didn't respect it was doomed to be bitten.

Thankfully, the soles of his boots were closest to the pit viper. The harder surface would provide him with some protection. However, if it went for his calves, the softer leather higher on his boots wouldn't stop those fangs from penetrating. The snake's large triangular head was a foot off the ground as the rest of its body coiled, preparing to strike.

This was what he got for not paying attention to his surroundings. Grandad would tear a strip off him if he got himself bitten. Maybe this was some sort of sign telling him to get his head out of the clouds when it came to one particular SEAL.

After a few moments, the rattlesnake began to back down and lowered its head until Ranger decided now was a good time to come back for him. At the thunder of hooves, the snake reared up and, before Bryan could move, bit him through the leather and into his calf.

"Shit," he yelled as he backed away, and the rattlesnake took off in the opposite direction.

Bryan didn't bother taking off his boot to look at the wound. He was a good hour's ride from the ranch house and needed to get to the medical center to receive antivenom. Time was of the essence, so he stood, got back on Ranger, and set off at a run heading home. His leg was already burning where he'd been bitten, and in time, would spread even higher. With the antivenom, he'd likely make a full recovery. Without it, the bite could be fatal.

As he honed in on the quickest direction to go, Bryan couldn't help but wonder, is fate getting what you deserve or deserving what you get, because on either count, he'd been failing miserably from a young age and wanted to know what he'd done to piss off karma.

If it weren't for bad luck, he'd have none at all. From broken bones, lowering beef prices, machines breaking down, drought, and even losing his parents. Maybe it was best to let the whole Shaw situation play out and then get his head on straight.

Maybe.

***

Shaw

Sweat dripped down Shaw's face as he looked at what they'd accomplished. He and Spence had been at it for over three hours, and the old paint was finally stripped off the side of the house. He made it down his ladder and took a long look back. There was something pleasing about finishing a job that they'd been putting off.

The crinkle of a chip bag had him turning to Spence. "You better stash those barbeque chips before Rick and Roman arrive tomorrow, or you'll never hear the end of it."

"I'm eating the evidence as we speak." Spence laughed before biting down on the crispy treat.

"What time do you figure we'll be heading out for LA on Thursday?"

"Early. We have a seven o'clock flight to catch," Spence answered before crumpling up his finished bag. "Only four more to go."

"Four more bags of chips? You might have a problem, my friend."

Spence laughed and threw the garbage in the trash can they'd been using to pick up the old paint scraps. Shaw still couldn't see what Spence saw in the short, bossy assistant, but he respected his friend's choice even if it beat the shit out of him how the two would gel. A special ops communications specialist with a slew of behind-the-scenes contacts coupled with an outlandish, bull-headed, mouthy man who'd invaded their home several times a month.

Okay, Shaw found the man annoying, but he was trying. Sort of.

"Looking good back here," Fletch said as he came around the corner. "We should be able to get this painted before you two head out."

Shaw figured the same. It gave them five days to paint, which should be plenty of time. Fletch gave Spence a look followed by a nod toward the other side of the house.

"Subtle," Shaw groaned at Fletch as Spence walked away. "What have I done now to piss you off?"

Fletch looked sheepishly at the ground. That was new. "Look, I'm sorry I've been behaving like an asshole."

Shaw's head snapped up. "Excuse me. I don't think I heard you correctly."

Fletch grinned. "I said I was sorry. I shouldn't have assumed the worst when it came to you and my brother."

"You mean I'm not out to fuck him and leave him?" Although Shaw tried hard not to let on, Fletch's suspicions had hurt him.

Fletch cringed but nodded his head. "I should've known better, man. We've been through hell and back together and you've always had my six. I'm truly sorry."

"Forgiven, man. I know how important Kyle is to you." Shaw smiled and slapped Fletch on the shoulder. "Besides, I'd never subject him to someone like me." He may have feelings for Kyle, but those would remain his own.

Fletch gave him a strange look, but it was gone in an instant when the man of the hour came around the corner in his wheelchair under his own speed. Though Julia wasn't far behind.

"Hey, Kyle. Come to see my amazing paint stripping skills?" Shaw laughed as he waved at the wall.

Without missing a beat, Kyle replied, "How could I stay away when you've been going on about it for days?"

Fletch joined in on the laughter, wiping away his concerned expression. Shaw had been serious. He'd never inflict his screwed-up life on Kyle, who deserved much better.

"The real reason I came looking for you was to ask if the offer was still open."

"Offer?" Fletch said, earning him a stern look from his brother. "Right, sorry."

Shaw knew what Kyle was asking and didn't delay in sharing, "You want to try riding one of Bryan's horses?"

"Yeah."

"What? You can't be serious. You're not getting on a horse. What if you fall?"

"Dude, Bryan and I won't leave his side. I swear it. We'd never let anything happen to him." Damn, Fletch. His protectiveness over his brother blanked his brain. When had Shaw ever abandoned Fletch's six?

"What if I like it? What if it makes me happy? There are a whole lot of 'what-ifs' in my world right now, and I refuse to allow them to stop me from living," Kyle said, his tone confident.

Shaw had known if Kyle took a couple of days to think about the offer, he'd see how much fun it could be, as well as good exercise. Shaw was overjoyed Kyle was going to get off the property and out in the world again.

"If you want to go, I'll make it happen," Shaw assured him.

"Is there any chance we can go before you leave for LA?" Kyle asked.

"I'll give Bryan a call and double-check, but I don't foresee a problem."

"Excellent." Fletch didn't look so convinced. "If you want to come with us, you're more than welcome to." Maybe that would reassure the big guy.

Fletch's shoulders lowered and he lost his puffed-up, protective look. "Thanks, man."

"Okay then, I'll make the call," Shaw said while pulling out his phone and hitting Bryan's contact. Shaw was surprised when Isaiah answered with, "Bryan Murray's phone."

"Isaiah? It's Shaw. Can I speak to Bryan?"

"I'm sorry, son, but he left his phone behind in his hurry to get to the medical center."

"Medical center? What happened? Is he okay?"

"He tangled with a rattler while out on a ride earlier today."

"Is he still there?"

"Yep, and I'm getting worried he can't call to give me an update."

"I'm headed there right now. I'll call you."

"Thanks, Shaw."

He turned to find the others staring at him in concern.

"Is something wrong?" Kyle asked.

"Yeah. Bryan's been bit by a rattlesnake," he answered, running for the garden doors. "I have to get to the medical center."

His keys were hanging on one of the hooks inside the door, and once he had them, he turned to find Kyle behind him. "I hope Bryan is okay," he said, looking all kinds of worried, which touched Shaw, especially since he'd never met him. He figured Kyle's concern was based on how the news affected Shaw. The man's empathy had no bounds. How had such a man survived his psycho parents?

"Thanks, Kyle. Me too," he replied, and to those gathered around Kyle's chair. "I'll call with news."

Shaw was out the door, in his truck, and on the road in record time. He wasn't even sure how he managed to get to the medical center. The next thing he knew, he was pulling into the parking lot next to the emergency department. He had to get to Bryan.

Running through the emergency doors, he stopped the first person in scrubs who happened to be a nurse he knew. They'd met at Clancy's and she'd shared lots of local gossip, making them fast friends. "I'm looking for Bryan Murray. He came in with a rattlesnake bite."

"He's in treatment bay six, at the end of the hall."

"Thanks," he called as he headed down the hall. He was surprised and thankful she hadn't asked him if he was family. Small towns, another reason to love them. You knew your neighbors.

Shaw pulled back the curtain at bay six to find Bryan lying on a gurney. His left calf was bandaged, and he was hooked up to an IV, a second smaller bag hanging from the pole that looked empty. Bryan's eyes were closed, but his chest still expanded with every breath he took, relieving Shaw's worst fear.

"Excuse me," someone said from behind him, alerting Bryan to Shaw's presence.

Shaw moved out of the doctor's way as she walked into the room. Bryan's expression gave him away: shock and relief in equal measure were easy to read. Shaw couldn't blame him. He was shocked by his reaction, and hadn't had the time to process what it meant.

Without thinking, he'd acted on instinct. Someone he cared about was hurt, and he needed to help even though, logically, he knew there was nothing he could do.

"Shaw?" Bryan asked. "You coming in?"

That's when he realized he was still standing in the same spot holding the privacy drape. "Ah, yeah." *Smooth.*

The doctor reviewed information on her tablet while Shaw made his way to Bryan's bedside.

"How'd you know I was here?"

"I called to ask about taking Kyle out riding, and your grandad told me. You okay?"

"I'm having antivenom therapy. So it's a wait-and-see situation kinda. The sooner you get the antivenom after a snake bite, the better the outlook."

"How long did it take for you to get here?"

"Two hours."

"Is that good?"

"In Bryan's case it is," the doctor said. "According to your most recent bloodwork, the antivenom is doing its job by slowing further tissue damage. The bite area shows minor necrosis and will likely scar, but further damage is unlikely. Your walking should be unaffected, and you can likely return to your ranch duties in twenty-four to thirty-six hours. We want to keep you under observation for a minimum of twelve hours to ensure there are no complications."

"I don't think I'm going anywhere fast, doc. I'm exhausted."

"Yes, well, a pit viper bite can cause you to become lethargic, but now that the intervention was successful, that should clear up. The best thing you could do right now is rest. I'll return to check in on you in a little while."

The second she stepped out, Shaw asked, "Why didn't you call me?"

Bryan tilted his head on the pillow and looked at him like he sprung another head. "Because I don't have my phone, and why would I? We're not a couple."

That hurt, but it was true. This was the way Shaw had wanted things to be. Simple, uncomplicated, unattached, no promises, no worries. *Shit.* "Because I still care about you. I'm not some heartless fucker." Why was he getting so worked up? This was what he'd wanted.

"I never said you were, but I'm staying within the parameters of our agreement."

He made complete sense, which angered Shaw more. Yeah, they had an agreement. No commitment, no unnecessary contact outside their times together, and everything could end at any time. He'd made up the rules that were now biting him in the ass.

"I want you to call me if something happens."

"You want to change the agreement?"

Did he? "Yeah." That was a first. He'd never considered such a thing before.

"Done," Bryan said with a smile. "Now that that's cleared up, can you call my grandad to let him know I'll be fine and away for the night?"

"I'll call him and the team. They're worried about you."

"Thanks."

Shaw turned and left the room to make his calls. By the time he returned, Bryan was fast asleep. Shaw pulled up a chair, sat down alongside Bryan, and watched his lover sleep.

The entire time he sat there wondering what the hell had happened, and why.

CHAPTER SIX

Bryan

Bryan watched as Shaw's truck pulled in and parked in his usual spot. Bryan and his grandfather sat on the porch waiting for the trio to arrive. He'd chosen one of his gentlest mares for Kyle's introduction to horseback riding.

He'd suggested Kyle try to ride one of their horses since his grandad rode regularly and had been in a wheelchair for over twenty-five years.

Shaw jumped out of the driver's seat, smiling from ear to ear, and winked at Bryan, making his pulse speed up. Fletch got out on the other side and opened the passenger door of the quad-cab. As soon as Shaw brought the wheelchair out of the truck's bed, he set it up outside the door and proceeded to lift a man from the backseat.

The sight of Shaw carrying the handsome man brought out the strangest of feelings in Bryan. Not jealousy or anger. An unexpected feeling of joy and excitement that he shoved down as far as he could. *What the hell is wrong with me?* The sight of his lover carrying this other man he felt he knew from Shaw's stories, but had yet to meet, should not be setting off feelings associated with meeting a new prospective lover.

He turned his head to find his grandad watching him closely.

"What?"

"You tell me," he said with a grin.

"There's nothing to tell. We better go introduce ourselves," he grumbled before standing and walking down the porch stairs while Isaiah took the ramp. "He'll think we aren't neighborly."

A slight limp was the only reminder of his run-in with the rattlesnake, and as soon as he healed further, that would disappear. By the time they reached the visitors, Bryan had himself under control. He held out his hand to Fletcher. "Good to see you again. How's the sheriff these days?"

"Good to see you too. Elias is working too much, as usual, but I'll let him know you were asking about him, and thanks for having us out."

"We're looking forward to it," Bryan said before offering his hand to Kyle, who was now in his chair. "Nice to meet you, Kyle. I'm Bryan, and this is Isaiah, my grandad. Welcome to Double M Ranch."

Kyle smiled and took hold of his hand. "Thank you for inviting me." The zing that shot up Bryan's arm from the man's touch had only happened once before with one other man. His lover, who was standing by Kyle's side. *Shit.* "I'm happy you're recovering from that snake bite."

"Yeah. Me too. Hurt like a sonofabitch."

He noticed the slight change in Kyle's hold before Bryan released his hand and stepped out of the way so Isaiah could shake hands. When he backed up, he found himself in Shaw's arms. Bryan wasn't sure how to act with Shaw when other people were around. Was he supposed to play it cool and aloof, or familiar? He wasn't a real boyfriend even if the agreement had been slightly altered.

"Hello there," Shaw whispered in his ear. "I missed you. How's your leg?"

The moment the words left Shaw's mouth, he seemed to realize what he'd said, but he didn't take them back. Missing someone assumed there were emotions involved. Something more between them than great sex and the occasional beer at Clancy's.

"I missed you too." Bryan decided to go with the truth. "And the leg's improving every day."

Bryan looked into Shaw's pale blue eyes and swore he could see the wheels turning in his lover's brain when they were jolted apart by Kyle's shocked tone. "You ride all the time?" His voice was filled with awe as he shook Isaiah's hand even faster.

"Damn right. I may have lost my legs, but not what makes me who I am. I'm a rancher, same as my father and his father before him. I exchanged two legs for four, and those four are a hell of a lot faster than I ever was."

"How?" Kyle asked, and his expression changed immediately. "I'm sorry, I shouldn't have asked that."

"Why the hell not?" Isaiah asked. "That's why you're here, right? To learn to ride. You can ask me anything,"

Kyle's face lit up, and he looked like he'd been given a great gift. "Thank you, sir."

Bryan couldn't help but smile. This was what he had hoped would happen once Kyle met his grandad. He'd see firsthand what was possible even if he was stuck in that wheelchair for longer than he'd hoped. Shaw's arm brushed against his and lingered there, but no words were spoken as Kyle looked over, his piercing blue eyes bright with burgeoning tears he quickly brushed away. His brilliant smile was thanks enough for Bryan.

After several moments Shaw said, "You've done a good thing here, babe. Thank you."

"Kyle is welcome here at the ranch anytime," Bryan said loud enough so Kyle could hear it.

"Let's get this show on the road," Isaiah shouted. "We're burning daylight." Leave it to his grandad to move things along.

Shaw pushed Kyle's chair, and Bryan walked alongside them. Fletch and Isaiah were up ahead, walking toward the corral where his grandad's horse, Starlight, stood waiting along with Missy, the horse he'd chosen for Kyle.

It all felt so normal and right. He was going to hell for even thinking what he was thinking. He was already in a noncommitted relationship of sorts, so why not be attracted to a second person? He was such an idiot, or glutton for punishment.

When he looked over at Shaw, his eyes were glued on Kyle as if waiting for a request or any sign of discomfort. He didn't know if Shaw realized how focused he was on the handsome man. There was no way to hide that amount of care and concern.

"There she is, Kyle," Isaiah hollered while pointing at the rig they'd created to help Grandad reach the saddle on Starlight. It wasn't pretty, but it worked. "Old beast here has been giving me a lift for over a decade, thanks to my grandson."

Bryan watched Kyle's face for any reaction as they neared the device he'd created. It wasn't much, some PVC pipe, wood, and odds and ends, really, along with a small 12 horsepower lawnmower engine. He'd worked his ass off getting it to work properly, and to make sure it was safe. Sure, they could have bought some commercial version, but every cent went into keeping the ranch afloat, so there was no need to buy it if he could make it.

"It looks like it can lift a horse, not put you on one," Kyle commented as he took in the large plastic pipes Bryan had used to create the supports for the seat that lifted a person to get on the saddled horse.

"Yeah. I gave it plenty of strength. I wanted to make sure it was sturdy and reliable when Grandad was on it." Bryan's greatest fear was something happening to his grandad. He'd lost his parents, and Isaiah was his only immediate family left.

"It looks plenty safe," Fletch stated after a quick inspection.

"And that there is Missy, my calmest mare. She won't let anything happen to you," Bryan said as he pointed at the bay-colored horse tied up to the fence, waiting patiently.

"Can I meet her first?" Kyle asked, looking a bit overwhelmed at the size of Missy.

"Anything you want," Bryan told him. Then Shaw pushed Kyle closer to the fence. "She's a gentle girl, you'll see."

Kyle looked up at him with absolute trust. "She's beautiful," he said while holding out the palm of his hand so Missy could take a long sniff. "I've never been near a horse before. I'm more of a city boy. Her nose is so soft."

"You don't know what you're missing, young man," Isaiah said as he joined them. "The spirit of a horse is unmatched by any animal. No one can convince me otherwise."

Bryan reached into his pocket and pulled out a sugar cube. "Here, give Missy this. She'll love you forever."

Kyle held the cube in the palm of his hand, and Missy didn't miss a beat. Her big tongue poked out, and after a quick taste test, her lips wrapped around the sugar cube, and she nibbled it into her mouth. Bryan smiled. Old Missy was a softy. He could tell she and Kyle would get along fine.

"Ready to give this a try?" Fletch asked his brother.

Kyle gave the horse another once-over before nodding and saying, "Let's do this."

***

Kyle

Kyle watched as Isaiah strapped himself into the machine Bryan had built. Kyle was still a bit unsure of all the moving parts, but instinctively he trusted the handsome cowboy. He wouldn't put his grandad in harm's way, so Kyle believed he'd be safe. That trust, the sense he had that nothing bad would ever happen to him, he also felt about the handsome Navy SEAL who'd been his constant companion from the moment Kyle was rescued.

Sure, fresh outta the closet, and I'm lusting after two unattainable men. What's wrong with me? Don't I have enough to deal with? He wondered if he'd kept this part of himself tucked away for too long, and now that he was out, every man was fair game? He didn't know the rules since he really didn't date many women for obvious reasons, and he was uncertain of himself in general. Being hobbled by his injuries and stuck in this damn wheelchair didn't make him a candidate for new lover of the year.

Before getting too worked up, he realized his attraction wasn't buckshot. He wasn't attracted to the other men on his brother's team or any of the male doctors he'd seen since being rescued. Hell, in truth, he'd never been so wholly attracted to anyone until now. It didn't matter. Nothing would ever happen.

Why these two? Maybe if he were still the person he used to be, he'd have a chance. He'd once been a confident entrepreneur, a leader of a highly successful resource company he'd created from the ground up, instead of the coward he'd become. The assured, poised person he used to be was gone forever. Even if he did regain use of his legs, he was damaged goods. He needed to learn how to deal with that reality. If he ever could.

"Kyle?" Shaw's voice penetrated the fog from the dark place his mind had visited. "You okay?"

Kyle looked up at Shaw's concerned face and snapped back into the present. "Yeah. Why?"

"We've been talking to you, and you haven't heard a word. What's up? If you're having second thoughts, that's okay. We can slow down," Bryan said, concern evident in his tone.

Shit. Kyle found himself getting lost in his thoughts more often recently, and he wasn't sure it was a good sign.

"Sorry," he rushed to say and followed up with a plausible explanation. "I was thinking about my therapists and what they would say about this." *There. A good, plausible lie.*

"They thought it was a great idea," Shaw threw out as if he knew what they'd said.

"You called them?" Kyle asked. Did they tell Shaw how badly his PT was going?

"Of course, I did," Shaw answered. "I didn't want to do anything that could potentially harm your recovery."

Fletcher looked away, confirming he was involved somehow.

Kyle wasn't sure if he should be upset or happy they'd gone above and beyond to make sure he was safe without consulting him or telling him. Before deciding which side of the coin to fall on, Isaiah turned the key and brought the claw-like lift to life.

He grabbed ahold of what appeared to be a joystick and said, "I'll show you how it's done, son."

Up he went smooth as silk as the hydraulics did their job. He stopped, and the entire arm swung out when he reached a height taller than the fence posts then hovered inside the corral. Bryan quickly jumped over the railing and led Starlight between two sets of steps below his grandad. As Isaiah was lowered to the saddle, Bryan stood on the steps and guided his legs around the sides of Starlight before the seat tipped forward slightly, allowing Isaiah to slide onto the saddle with ease. He used leather straps attached to the front and back of the saddle to hold him in place since he didn't have the use of his leg muscles to grip the horse. Bryan went around Starlight and set each of his grandad's feet into the stirrups. Then Isaiah was off trotting around the ring with a huge smile on his face.

He looked so free up there. If Isaiah wanted to go left, they went left, the same with the right. Kyle hadn't had control over his direction in what felt like forever. He was pushed everywhere, which wasn't the same thing.

"Ready to give this a shot?" his brother asked as he drew closer.

Kyle could see the joy on Isaiah's face and wanted so badly to feel that way again. "Oh yeah. As Isaiah would say, 'Let's get this show on the road.'"

Things moved pretty quickly after that, and soon Kyle found himself buckled into Bryan's machine.

"This is how you control where you go, much like a video game," Bryan said as he leaned forward and pointed to the joystick. "You have the side-to-side buttons, and the forward is for when you want to go higher, and back is down."

"That makes sense," Kyle stated calmly, even with his stomach churning.

"You wanna give it a test drive?" Shaw asked.

Having the two of them hovering so close made his head swim. The smell of leather, earth, and sweat was a heady combination from these two Adonises.

He needed some air. "I'll give it a try." Kyle pushed forward on the joystick, and he went up and away from the temptations below.

When he reached as high as the claw could go, he pushed the left button and went out over the ring. It was such a smooth ride for a machine that appeared more fitting on one of those battle robots that fought in a different kind of ring.

Kyle was beginning to figure out that Bryan wasn't much for the show and looks of things, but more about fulfilling a need, as well as safety, and comfort for those needing to use it. He found it reassuring and charming about the handsome cowboy.

"How's it feel?" Bryan hollered up at him.

How did he feel? Kyle looked around at this new height, and he could see out into the pasturelands and trees beyond the immediate area. It was stunning scenery: bright blue birds flew in and out of view around the brush and trees, while in the distance, he could make out what he thought might be longhorn cattle, but they were too far away to see properly. The Texas sun shone down on him, and the sky was deep blue and endless.

"Beautiful," Kyle answered without really thinking about the question.

"I agree," Bryan said with a grin as Shaw smiled wide beside him.

Kyle felt heat working its way up his neck, but quickly turned away and said, "I'm ready to give Missy a shot."

Bryan climbed over the fence to bring Missy around. Kyle made practice turns to get a feel for the controls so he wouldn't end up hurting Missy by accidentally hitting her on his way down.

"I'm ready," he said, and in a much lower voice, "I think."

Considering he'd never been near a horse when he had the use of his legs gave him pause while he lowered down over the top of a thousand pounds of Missy. This was insane.

Before he lost his nerve, Bryan hitched Missy to a post and climbed up the stairs to face him.

"It's okay if you'd rather stop," he said.

Kyle wasn't doing a good job of hiding his emotions. Boots on the opposite set of stairs had him turning left to find Shaw coming up to the other side of him.

"How are you doing?" Shaw asked, his concern as evident as Bryan's.

"I want to ride Missy," Kyle told them. And he honestly did. "But what if she gets spooked and takes off or today's the day she decides to try showjumping over the fence?" Okay, he was being illogical. Missy looked more ready to take a nap than jump over anything.

"We can stop at any time," Bryan assured him. "You've already gone a long way."

"How about Bryan and I walk on either side of you and keep hold of her harness. She won't be going anywhere we don't want her to go," Shaw suggested.

Bryan nodded in agreement. "No way I'd send you out there alone."

Kyle could feel his stress lowering at the new plan. "Okay. I can do this."

"You can do anything you put your mind to, brother," Fletcher said from where he and Isaiah were waiting.

With his brother's unwavering faith in him, Kyle stowed away his nerves and concentrated on the task at hand: getting in the saddle.

"I'm ready."

"I'll hold Missy still while Shaw leads you down."

"Okay," Kyle answered while nodding. He could do this.

Shaw waited until Bryan was ready and took control of the joystick. "We won't let anything happen to you. Promise."

"I trust the two of you," Kyle said without having to think about it, and he truly did.

"Good," Shaw said with a wink, dispelling the last of Kyle's nerves.

Slowly and methodically, he was lowered down until his legs were on either side of Missy. The next step would be to release the seatbelt holding him onto the chair, and then he'd be in the saddle.

"Whenever you're ready," Bryan said as if he had all day to decide.

Kyle looked down at Missy, who was munching away on a small pile of apples, looking about as dangerous as a feather. *He could do this. He could do this.* The mantra rang through his head as he reached for the release button, and with one final silent prayer, he pushed it.

***

Shaw

Shaw watched as Kyle made his choice and released the seatbelt. The courage this man possessed still had the power to amaze him. Gently, he guided Kyle into the saddle using his strength as Bryan made sure his feet were securely in the stirrups. They tightened the straps around Kyle's body on either side of the saddle and secured him in place.

Missy hadn't bothered to stop eating throughout the process. The horse was as calm as a sniper at scope one thousand yards out. Shaw never doubted his lover would pick the perfect horse for Kyle.

The one thing he hadn't expected was the chemistry between Kyle and Bryan, though he couldn't say he was jealous per se. He and Bryan weren't "together," and they hadn't made any promises to each other, so he discounted its similarity to his parents' behavior. Actually, he found himself more intrigued than anything else. The two were trying to hide their obvious connection, but Shaw saw through them easily enough. Perhaps he could see it because he was close to both men. Who knew, but at least to him, it was plain to see.

"There you go, Kyle. You're securely strapped on. There is no chance of you falling off," Bryan said as he gathered the reins and handed them to Kyle.

"What am I supposed to do with these?" Kyle asked, his eyes big and his brows up. "I don't know how to drive one of these."

Shaw couldn't help but chuckle. "Ride, not drive. Don't worry, we'll be leading Missy around for you. No 'driving' necessary."

Kyle nodded, but he was still chewing on his bottom lip, which Shaw knew was a sign the man was unsure. He'd noticed the trait long ago, and every time Kyle chewed his lip, it did something to Shaw he refused to look at too closely.

"Okay, I'm holding you to it," Kyle stated.

"I swear I won't do anything to cause you harm," Bryan said with absolute conviction. "You have my word on it."

Shaw could feel the truth of Bryan's words, and apparently, so could Kyle. "Let's give this a shot." Kyle's back straightened, and his eyes were focused on Missy. He gave her a gentle pat. "You're a good girl, Missy."

As if sensing Kyle's acceptance, the mare lifted her head and sniffed the air, no longer focused on her treats. Slowly, they led her out from between the stairs and into the ring. It felt like everyone was holding their collective breaths in anticipation.

Kyle looked down between the two of them on either side of Missy for a moment, and Shaw got the distinct impression Kyle's checking on him and Bryan meant more than the horse ride. He looked over to find Bryan staring at Kyle, looking for signs of the slightest discomfort, and seemed ready to jump into action.

They completed one lap around the ring before stopping to make sure Kyle was still into it.

"How's it feel?" Fletch asked as they neared the fence where he and Isaiah, on his horse, waited.

"Scary, exciting, overwhelming, freeing, and all the words in between." Kyle laughed and broke out into a smile. "I think I like it."

Shaw felt his heart skip a beat at his and Bryan's happy smiles. He expected to feel some sort of guilt and shame for the thoughts going through his head, but he didn't. All he felt was an intense need to take care of these two men and protect them. This wasn't normal. Or was it? Was he the product of his upbringing? Maybe he was more like his parents than he thought—he'd never be satisfied with one partner.

He was leaving tomorrow for LA and hoped a little space would give him time to think clearly because his head wasn't on straight, and he needed to fix his thinking. Everything he believed and fought against was coming back around. Hell, he'd even told Bryan he'd missed him. He never held on to attachments long enough to miss anyone.

His world was changing, and he wasn't sure he was prepared for the consequences.

CHAPTER SEVEN

Shaw

"Seriously? This is what you consider inconspicuous?" screeched a voice Shaw was quickly beginning to dislike. "They're ten feet tall. They'll stand out."

When he and Spence arrived in LA, they were surprised to discover it wasn't an ambassador they would be guarding but the ambassador's eighteen-year-old daughter. As if things couldn't get worse, she wanted to go to a concert while she was in town. Her father would be working during the entire stay while Shaw and Spence played babysitter. *Great.*

However, a job was a job, and they'd do what they were hired to do whether the client wanted them there or not. But that voice was another matter entirely.

"Giselle, you know your father has instructed you go nowhere without your bodyguards while we're in Los Angeles. This isn't up for debate." The ambassador's assistant, Bing, waved the teenager away as if she were a fly, which rubbed Shaw the wrong way.

"We are trained to protect you for your safety," Spence said, trying to help explain their presence and make it more palatable.

The scowl he received from Giselle should've had his buddy rolling around on the floor in pain. So much for helping.

"I just want to be normal for once. Go to movies and malls like other teenagers," she whined. "It's not my fault he's some stupid ambassador. Why do I have to live like a prisoner?"

"As I have told you numerous times, you're not a prisoner, but you are at risk of kidnapping as a way of hurting the Moroso Government, and we can't allow that to happen. Your father is the ambassador for our country, and your uncle is president. This puts you at risk. You should be happy to be so well cared for." Moroso was an oil-rich nation on the other side of the world.

The assistant wasn't earning any points as far as Shaw was concerned. He had an officious manner, and he treated the girl like she was a simpleton. "We will remain as inconspicuous as possible given the situation." Where the hell did that come from? Shaw hadn't intended to say a thing, but you know what they say about best-laid intentions.

Giselle looked over at them in frustration. "See that you do."

And right back to hating the sound of her voice. He should've known better. To her, they were nothing more than pains in the ass who'd been hired to be her living shields. He couldn't say he hadn't felt that way at times, but, as always, he'd do his job to the best of his ability.

"Fine. I want to go to Rodeo Drive," she ordered before storming away toward the front door.

Shaw and Spence dutifully followed without saying a word. They knew the score. By the time they reached the lobby of the Beverly Wilshire hotel, their black, bulletproof SUV had pulled up out front. Spence led the way out of the building and scanned the area before opening the back door, the signal for all clear.

"What's wrong with you guys?" Giselle put her hands on her hips and tilted her head, her enormous sunglasses hiding most of her scrunched-up face. "We don't need to take the car. We only have to walk across the street."

Spence said, "We need to be able to get away quickly if there's trouble."

"You think there'll be trouble shopping on Rodeo Drive? You guys are nuts."

"We're charged with keeping you safe, miss. We take our duty seriously," Shaw explained through gritted teeth. "Now please, get in the vehicle," he instructed in a low tone.

Whatever fight was left in her came through with her flounce. "Oh, all right," she said as she went straight into the vehicle as if she'd done it a million times before. The driver was part of the Moroso guard, and per Spence and Shaw's orders, he wasn't permitted to get out of the driver's seat. If there was trouble, he had to be ready to go at a moment's notice.

Once she was secured, Spence jumped into the front passenger's seat while Shaw sat in the back with Giselle. They pulled away from the curb and merged, went around the block, which took fifteen minutes. LA traffic. A nightmare.

Giselle was silently staring out the window, for which Shaw was grateful. He'd be lying if he said he didn't enjoy the quiet, but the sniffle that seeped into the SUV sucker-punched him. He could see how difficult this situation could be for a teenager looking for her independence.

As they turned onto Rodeo Drive, Giselle said, "I've changed my mind. Take me to one of those big-box stores I've heard so much about."

"Big box?" the driver asked.

Spence turned around in his seat. "You mean like Costco or Target?"

"Yes. Those are familiar names," Giselle said and flashed her first real smile since they'd met her. "I would like to go there."

Shaw pulled out his cell phone and searched for the nearest Target. "Looks like the safest location is on Santa Monica Boulevard and South Westgate."

"Got it," Spence replied before relaying the address to the driver, who plugged it into the GPS.

Shaw wondered why Giselle wanted to go someplace so vastly different than what he'd expected. Especially since she meant to start on Rodeo Drive. *Maybe she wants to go slumming with us normal folks?* Either way, he didn't care, and it was none of his business.

By the time they reached the store, the streetlights had begun turning on as the sun dipped low in the sky. Even he had to admit the sunsets in California were something to behold. The driver pulled up to the front of the store, and Spence got out first to survey the location. When he came back, he opened the back door.

"All looks secure in the immediate area," Spence said.

Shaw nodded, got out, and scanned the area again while waiting for Giselle to step out. When she did, they flanked her on their way into the store as the SUV moved a few feet forward to idle at the curb a few yards from the store's front entrance.

This store wasn't overly busy and there were six cashiers, one who didn't have a line in her lane. "This looks acceptable," Giselle said before walking over to cashier without the line. "I'd like to speak with the store manager."

The wide-eyed young cashier looked past Giselle and at the two of them. "Is this a robbery?" Shaw and Spence were dressed in jeans, button-down shirts, and jackets, but Shaw didn't think they looked like thugs. Maybe it was the gun bulge that had the kid worried.

"Would I ask for the manager, or come in with a ski mask on hiding my identity if all I wanted was your money?" Giselle asked while shaking her head. "The education system in this country leaves something to be desired."

After the cashier hustled away, Shaw said, "Unfortunately, many people working in these positions have to fear being robbed because it's a real threat."

"Why does your government not protect them?" Giselle demanded.

"They try. We have police and the military, but we can't be everywhere all the time," Shaw explained.

"The two of you are former police?" she asked.

"No. Military. Navy SEALs," Shaw stated.

"You quit?"

"No. We retired," Spence told her. They'd never quit anything they'd started.

"And yet you're both still protecting others from danger," Giselle observed.

"We're good at what we do," Shaw assured her.

"I bet you are." Something changed in her expression, but it was gone as quickly as it came.

Before he could answer, the cashier and a woman who looked to be in her fifties came walking up to them. The woman wore a bright red blouse that matched her cheeks.

"Hello," the woman said while holding out her hand. "I'm Mary, the store manager. How can I help you?" Her nervousness was apparent.

Giselle took hold of the offered hand and shook it. "Very nice to meet you, Mary. I've come to you today because I need your help with a special mission."

Shaw expected her to ask to close the store for her private shopping pleasure or something equally as cliché, but would admit to being shocked when Giselle revealed what she wanted.

"I wish to make a substantial purchase and donate it to a charity named Ronald McDonald House. I require the entire children's and babies' sections of merchandise you have in the store. Can you facilitate that?" Giselle asked as if that were an everyday request. Perhaps in her world it was.

"Um," Mary began but seemed at a loss for words. To tell the truth, so was Shaw.

Giselle carried on as if she hadn't just given the woman the shock of her life. "I have been in contact with a representative with this charity who has confirmed the need for children's clothing." Giselle pulled out a piece of paper and handed it to the manager. "If you contact this gentleman, he will arrange for the items to be picked up and taken to their distribution facility. They intend to make care packages for families with children in hospitals."

Mary's hands shook as she took the piece of paper. "Is this for real?"

"I assure you it is," Giselle confirmed as she pulled out a black Amex card from her bag. "I will cover whatever cost for labor is necessary for those who wish to help with the donation."

Shaw shared a confused look with Spence. This was not the shopping spree they'd expected to be going on today. An eighteen-year-old with a credit card without a limit was more likely to plough through the high-end store on Rodeo.

"Make sure to include the diapers and all the stuff to go with them. Parents at these places shouldn't have to worry about any of it," Giselle added as she pulled out a list and began checking things off. "Diaper cream, wipes, powder...everything."

A slow smile brightened Mary's face as it began to sink in. "Ron, Jason, please lock the doors. We have a special order." She turned to Giselle. "Excuse me. I have to call my regional director to let her know what's going on."

"Thank you, take all the time you need."

"Whom should I say is making the donation?" Mary asked.

Giselle pulled out a business card. "The people of Moroso."

One thing Shaw had to say about the day, he'd been distracted enough to've back-burnered what he was thinking and feeling about the Bryan and Kyle situation.

***

Bryan

Bryan watched as Fletch's truck pulled up to the ranch house much the same as it had four days earlier. The only difference was today there was no Shaw, who was away on a job. Bryan walked up to the truck to find Kyle smiling in the passenger's seat while waiting for

Fletch to pull out his wheelchair from behind the truck's second row of seats.

"'Morning, Bryan," Fletch said with a wave as he neared. "Looks like it's going to be a good day for another lesson."

While still riding Missy, Kyle had arranged to come out for a second ride before finishing his first. His excitement was palpable. The man had more strength than he gave himself credit for, and Bryan had decided to make it his mission to show Kyle the truth of who he still was. Shaw had shared Kyle's past life as a successful entrepreneur and CEO, and it didn't take a genius to figure out the man was depressed by what'd been done to him—by his parents, for fuck's sake.

"Hey, Bryan," Kyle called out as he opened the passenger door. "Missy ready for round two?"

"You bet. This time around, I'll show you how we saddle her and get her ready for a ride." Bryan figured the more someone knew about an animal's care, the more respect they'd have for the animal.

Kyle's eyes lit up. "That sounds perfect."

Fletch brought over the wheelchair and in one quick motion, he lifted his brother from the truck and placed him in the chair.

"Thanks for having Kyle out again," Fletch said. "I shouldn't be back any later than four this afternoon."

"No rush, there's lots to do and see on a ranch to keep us busy." He'd made sure to start his morning chores earlier so he'd have plenty of time to spend with Kyle.

"Great, have fun, bro," Fletch said as he squeezed his brother's shoulders. "Don't overdo it."

"Yeah, yeah, mother hen." Kyle rolled his eyes, making Fletch laugh as he walked back to his truck, and then drove away.

Kyle and Bryan were alone. Well, not really alone since Grandad was in the barn, and the ranch hands were about, well into their day's work.

"Ready to get started?" Bryan asked, feeling excited.

"You bet," Kyle said with conviction. "Where do we begin?"

"First in the barn here," he explained before coming up behind the wheelchair and pushing Kyle inside. "Isaiah's waiting on us to get the horses set for the ride we have planned."

"Ride? Where?" Kyle's voice was full of excitement.

"To check a few fence lines."

"Are you sure I'm ready for that?"

"It isn't too far away, and the land is even. Missy will have no problem, and the view will be a hell of a lot better than what you get from going 'round in circles in the ring."

Kyle's smile returned. "Sounds like fun. Thanks."

"Anytime. You're always welcome here."

"Are you sure I'm not an imposition?" Kyle asked, his happy tone subdued.

Bryan stopped pushing the wheelchair and came around the front of it before squatting to be at eye level with Kyle. "You could never be an imposition. Never think that."

Their gazes were locked, and Bryan couldn't pull himself away. The concern in Kyle's eyes was like a knife to his heart. It sucked he saw himself as an imposition or inconvenience. But Bryan understood. If he lost the use of his legs for more than a day, he'd be ornery to the point of impossible to be around.

"It's different now," Kyle muttered. "I can't contribute like I used to. People have to bring me things and take me places even if they don't want to because of," he looked down at himself, "my legs. I'm like a third wheel or a dead weight. The albatross around everyone's neck."

Bryan was getting angry, and his need to protect this guy who'd suffered so much because he did the right thing was overpowering. "Did someone tell you that? Who was it? What'd they say?"

Kyle seemed shocked by Bryan's vehemence. "Whatcha going to do? Hunt them down to defend my honor?"

"If I have to."

Kyle's smile was small, but it was still a smile. "It wasn't anyone. I know how useless my body is."

"You are far from useless, and I'll show you." Bryan was more determined to prove his point.

"I'd like to see you try," Kyle jabbed, but Bryan could tell by the small smirk, the guy was kidding.

"You're on."

With Kyle's humor back in place, Bryan stood. "Do you know how to drive that thing?"

"The chair? Yeah. PT, man."

"Then I'll meet you in the barn." It took everything for Bryan to walk away, but he knew Kyle needed to feel in control of his life and useful. If Bryan saw Kyle was having trouble, of course, Bryan would help, but only then. Independence began now.

The moment he set foot in the barn, he raced to a nearby window to check on Kyle's progress, but he couldn't find him anywhere outside when he looked.

"Looking for me?" Kyle said from his side, making Bryan jump as he turned.

"Shit, man. You're fast. Why the hell aren't you pushing yourself around all the time?"

"I don't usually get the chance. My brother, *the SEAL*, likes to think he's helping."

"Well, around here, I expect you to get around on your own. Providing, if you need help, you have to swear, you'll tell me."

"I swear," Kyle said, and put up his fingers. "Scout's honor."

Bryan chuckled. "Good. Let's get to work."

They moved down the concrete lane between the stalls, which lined both sides of the barn, until they reached Missy's stall. There were a couple of bales of hay to the right of the stall door with a blanket laid over the top. On the post between the stalls was a hook on which hung a turnout halter and lead.

"Here she is," Bryan said, and Missy came over and stuck her big head out to have a look at her visitors.

Kyle dug through his jean pocket and produced three sugar cubes, catching Missy's attention. "Hello again, sweet girl," Kyle crooned as she lowered her head to her waiting treat.

"Smart move keeping the old girl happy." Bryan was delighted Kyle remembered Missy's favorite treat.

"Don't listen to him, Missy. You're not old. You're mature and stunning."

"Sorry, I didn't mean to offend you, Missy." Bryan played along.

"You're forgiven." Kyle laughed. "But remember, females are touchy about their age."

"Noted," Bryan agreed with a smile he couldn't tamp down. "I'll show you where we keep the tack and saddles."

Bryan crossed over to the opposite side of the barn where there was a large tack room at the far end. The moment he entered, the smell of worn leather filled the air. This was a repair room and storage all in one. Racks of saddles covered the far wall, while the bridles, bits, reins, stirrups, and blankets each had their places in the tack room. He liked to keep things tidy. Across the way was where they kept the feed, the liniments and such, as well as the barn's cleaning implements

"Wow, look at all this stuff," Kyle said as he rolled in.

"Tack."

"Tack?"

"Yeah. All the stuff you put on a horse to ride is called tack."

"Why?"

"It's short for tackle, and it's a reference to riding or directing domesticated horses."

"Okay, tack," Kyle agreed. "Here's where you keep all of it?"

"Yep. Each horse has a set of their own tack as well as spares in case something needs to be repaired or replaced."

"I get the feeling you don't replace a lot."

"Not if I can help it. Tack's expensive. Why replace it when you can fix it and get years more life out of it?"

"You're handy to have around, building the lift, and all," he waved his arm to the room, "this. I bet your grandad is proud of you."

Bryan chuckled. "Maybe once I got it all fine-tuned. Up until then, I'm sure Grandad had a few choice words, and none of them screamed proud," Bryan said. Working a ranch didn't go smoothly even when he knew what he was doing and he had help. The maxim "if something can go wrong it does,"applied here in spades.

"Oh no, what happened?" Kyle turned from a saddle Bryan had been repairing to look at him.

"One time, the lift got stuck and Grandad was high in the air. I had to call the fire department in to get him down."

"Ouch."

"Yeah, he didn't speak to me for three days." Bryan couldn't help but laugh at the sight of his grandad being carried down the ladder like a sack of potatoes. He could laugh about it now, but back then, he worried that he'd never be able to make the machine work properly.

"But you persevered and created a machine that allows him to do the one thing he loves: riding. You have to be proud of that."

"It needed doing, and I did it." Like most things around here.

"Humble and handsome," Kyle said, but the moment the words were out of his mouth, Bryan could tell Kyle had shocked himself. "What I mean is—"

"You think I'm handsome?"

"Have you looked in a mirror?"

Bryan felt the heat rise from his neck to his face where it settled on his cheeks. Shit, men don't blush.

"Here you two are. I was beginning to wonder what was keeping you," Grandad said as he rolled into the room.

"Hello, Mr. Murray," Kyle said. "It's good to see you again. Bryan was showing me where you keep all your tack."

"Was he now? Careful he doesn't rope you into mucking out a stall or two," Isaiah said with a wink.

"Might as well get Missy's gear," Bryan said without turning to face his grandad. He'd see the red on his face and be all over him like white on rice. "It's over here, Kyle."

Bryan led Kyle over to Missy's saddle. The bridle, reins, and the rest hung beside it. "Can you carry some of this?"

"You bet." Kyle rolled up close.

"Good," Bryan said before laying Missy's blanket and then the lighter tack on Kyle's lap before lifting the saddle and leading the way back to her stall. Bryan set up the saddle bar he'd recessed into the wall to keep it out of the way when not in use, and unloaded his cargo. Kyle held out the rest of the tack with a smile, and Bryan hung it up beside the saddle.

"Ready to learn how to saddle a horse?" Bryan asked. "Then, after our ride, we can curry her down, and then brush her out."

"Totally," Kyle said as Bryan opened Missy's stall.

CHAPTER EIGHT

Shaw

Shaw leaned against the wooden headboard in the adjoining bedroom to the ambassador's three-bedroom suite he and Spence were sharing. Close by if needed, but still managing to retain their, and their charge's, privacy.

Since Giselle was in for the night, they were off duty while the ambassador's personal bodyguards watched the halls and entrances. So far, nothing eventful had happened other than their client's mercurial behavior. One moment she was calm and reasonable, the next, she was spoiled and bratty. But even then, that behavior seemed to be at its worst when the ambassador's assistant was within earshot. Which made Shaw wonder what was going on between those two.

"I think we're in the twilight zone, buddy," Spence said as he came out of the bathroom from his shower. "Shit's going on around here, and that assistant needs a slap upside his head."

"Did you have a check in with our client before we got here?" Shaw asked though he doubted Spence wouldn't have done that from the start. Spence was their communications specialist. Information was his stock in trade, and he had connections far and wide. No one could stop him from getting information if he wanted it. He could call in a helicopter as easily as a pizza. Crazy mad skills.

"Yeah, I checked out the entire family as well as the state of play in Moroso. Nothing stuck out as wrong aside from the usual backroom deals and proximity to much more powerful countries in the Middle East. I'll give it another shot tonight because I agree, that assistant, Bing… The dude rubs me the wrong way."

"Same here. Shifty-eyed asshole. More than once, I caught him whispering while on his cell. It may've been on the up and up, but he hung up fast every time I got within earshot." It'd been bothering Shaw for the last couple of days, along with the overt animosity between Bing and Giselle.

Spence went to his messenger bag and pulled out his laptop as well as a portable satellite dish, and set himself up on the desk by the window. His laptop looked like a piece of old junk for a reason. If it seemed to be a personal POS, no one would have any interest in it. However, its insides were state-of-the-art plus. Spence could set up an entire outpost with a few keystrokes. Knowing how valuable an asset the laptop was, Spence made sure it had all the protections to keep its capabilities hidden. Without knowing the four-step authentication, the machine would run as if it were an old device running on outdated software, which would present fake files and bogus search histories.

Only Spence knew how to unleash its true power through a multilevel encrypted security system that Shaw couldn't crack. Spence had tested it out on the team and no one could get through Spence's protection. Shaw would be surprised if there wasn't a self-destruct button or kill switch.

"Whatever Bing's hiding, it won't be a secret for long. Mind putting on another pot of coffee?" Spence asked.

"Sure." Shaw stood and made his way over to the typical hotel setup of a coffee machine, sugars, creams, and spoons. Their room was basic compared to the suite next door, and he figured this was where the hired help stayed. Tens of thousands of hours of training. More successful ops than any other team in SEAL history, and they didn't even rate a Nespresso machine.

After handing Spence his coffee, Shaw lay down on his bed and pulled out his cell phone as Spence began typing away on his keyboard like a caffeinated squirrel. Shaw had no doubt Spence would dig up every last detail on Bing before the night was through.

Shaw opened his phone and saw a message waiting for him in a group chat. He opened it and immediately smiled when he saw who it was from. Bryan and Kyle had created a three-way chat so they could communicate while he was out of town. Happiness filled him as nothing else had ever done before. Which was insane. He hadn't bothered to examine his whole reaction to the three of them and what might be happening between them. He shoved it down where it belonged. What he and Bryan had was only temporary. It had to be. And Kyle? That was a complication he couldn't even contemplate.

Kyle: Hey guys. I hope it's fine that I've set up this chat. I figured it would be a good way to stay in touch.

Bryan: All right by me. I think it's a great idea.

That's where the conversation stopped, and it became apparent they were waiting for him to weigh in before continuing with the conversation. It was well past eleven p.m., surely they'd both be asleep by now, but that didn't stop him from answering.

Shaw: I agree. Great idea. How'd your horse ride go?

He shut the phone, not expecting an answer until tomorrow, and stared at the ceiling, wondering and hoping everything went well. Kyle needed to have control over more aspects of his life. If the unthinkable happened and he couldn't walk again, he needed to know life held options that wouldn't hamper his ability to do more great and wonderful things.

The slight vibration of his phone alerted him to a new message, and he'd never opened his phone so fast about something personal.

Bryan: He's a pro now.

Kyle: Funny. I still have no idea what the hell I'm doing, smartass.

Shaw: What are you two doing up this late?

Bryan: Watching tube.

Kyle: Practicing riding in my head.

Bryan: Ha. For real, Kyle was great. We went out to part of the west pasture to check the fence line.

Shaw: You went out to the pasture? Kyle, that's amazing.

Kyle: It wasn't too far, but I didn't fall off. I'll take it as a win.

Bryan: Don't sell yourself short. The next time we'll go a little farther.

Shaw: When's the next time?

Kyle: Wednesday, if Bryan still has time.

Bryan: I'll make time. How's everything in LA?

Shaw: Interesting. We're assigned to watch over the teenage daughter of an ambassador.

Kyle: That's...different.

Bryan: How hard is the daughter to protect?

Shaw: Her mood swings can give you whiplash, but her charity work is impressive.

Bryan: Stay safe.

Shaw: I will.

Kyle: Promise.

Shaw: Promise. See you both soon. Sack time.

Bryan: Right.

Kyle: 'Night.

Shaw closed the chat and went back to staring at the ceiling, concerned it might be too late to make a clean break. He was in deep, and he wasn't sure how it happened.

He could bow out and allow Bryan and Kyle the chance to make an honest go of it. Neither of them *really* knew him, and would probably thank him if they did. Those two had staying power. He didn't. But could he survive losing them?

He didn't trust his instincts, especially when his emotions were all over the place. This was why he didn't do relationships. This was why he avoided commitment. He barely recognized himself. But was that a bad thing?

Did he like this new version, and could he be what they needed?

***

Giselle

Giselle watched as the shadow of footsteps passed by her bedroom door before pulling out her cell. During her trips to the American stores' electronics departments, she'd had a chance to procure what she'd been looking for. Then earlier this evening, she'd had the opportunity to put the inconspicuous tiny device in place when she'd gone to wish her father good night. Now all that was left was to get some answers for the strange goings-on these past six months.

She'd followed the instructions and set up the app associated with the tiny device. Then she turned on the video and voice relays before sitting back to watch the show. Her father and Bing appeared on screen from inside the office. Her father sat behind his desk, and Bing sat in one of the two chairs set in front of it. Both were busy reading documents with only the sound of pages turning in the background.

Not exactly sizzling content, but she refused to turn it off until the room was empty. The sight of her father's assistant made her skin crawl. It wasn't that the man had ever made a move on her or anything like that, but there was something she found abhorrent about his presence, especially when he was near her father. The feeling came from deep inside her, and she couldn't ignore it. Several minutes later, her father yawned and set down the papers.

"It has been a long day, Bing. Let us finish this in the morning before we have our video meeting with Senator Reynolds's representatives tomorrow afternoon to discuss our offer further." Her father stood, and so did Bing.

"Yes, sir. I will continue examining the contracts so I'm able to advise you of any concerns in the morning." Bing bowed as he spoke.

"Good. You are truly a faithful servant of Moroso. How is Giselle enjoying her time in Los Angeles?"

"Other than complaining profusely about her need for bodyguards, she appears to be flittering away her days shopping and attending notable sightseeing locations. The girl is unprepared to take her place and perform her duty to the people of Moroso."

Giselle growled low in her throat, but it was exactly what she wanted Bing to believe, so she'd done her job well. *Gullible piece of shit.*

"She is young and deserves to enjoy her youth. Soon enough, the weight of responsibility will become her cloak." Her father's faith in her made Giselle happier than she'd been in a long time.

"Yes, sir." Since her father was facing the opposite direction, he didn't see the bastard roll his eyes.

"I'll take my leave, and we will discuss what you've found in the morning. Sleep well, my friend."

Giselle bristled at "friend." Bing was no friend to her father, and she wished he could see that. Until he did, it was her job to protect him, and she took that job seriously.

"Sleep well, Ambassador Maas," Bing said before bowing again to her father's retreating figure as he walked out of the office.

Giselle waited and watched as her father's footsteps went by her closed door and on to his bedroom, then listened for him to close the door behind him. She turned her attention to the man she despised, who walked over to the office door and locked it. Interesting.

Her stomach turned when Bing walked past the chair he'd been sitting in and headed straight for her father's chair. Bastard. He leaned back and lifted his feet onto the desk like he owned the place. Giselle had been right not to trust the smarmy guy. That's why she behaved like a spoiled brat when Bing was around to throw him off and make him believe she was none the wiser.

There was something innately evil about him. She'd been told her mother held such a gift as seeing someone as they truly were. She had died giving birth to Giselle, and her guilt over that loss never left her. That's why she needed to protect her father. He had sought her mother's counsel when faced with unknown people and situation, and without her, he was vulnerable.

A low, maniacal laugh played over her phone as Bing made himself at home. She had the feeling this wasn't the first time the jerk had sat in her father's chair, probably dreaming of his self-importance instead of being a servant to the people of their country. Giselle had always suspected him of ulterior motives, but without proof, she was dead in the water.

"C'mon, asshole, give me something to work with," she growled low as not to be heard by her father's bodyguards. She wasn't a fool. She was recording Bing's every move.

As if he were taking requests, Bing sat up and pulled out his cell, touched the screen, and leaned back with the phone pressed to his ear.

"Bing here. Don't worry. He's turned in for the evening. The dolt suspects nothing."

Giselle would've loved to know who he was speaking to.

"Of course, I've been careful. The old man has no clue he's about to set off a chain reaction that will see the end of the Maas family rule over Moroso. With one simple signature, it will be done, and by the time he figures it out, it will be too late for him and his brother, President Maas. Then we can finally be together again." He paused, listening. "No, there are no concerns. I brought in outside bodyguards, and Giselle is nothing more than a nuisance. What about us, don't you miss me?" Bing whined. "I miss you."

Oh my god, she was witnessing an illicit romance. What the hell?

"You do? Tell me more about what you intend to do when we're reunited." Bing undid the button on his pants and slid his hand down. Great, she'd have to sit through a jerk-off session, though she was grateful the desk hid the lower half of his body. Her face twisted in disgust as he violently pumped his cock to whatever was being said on the other end of the line. She could honestly say she hadn't expected this when she set up the camera.

A sharp knock on the office door had Bing buttoning his pants and hanging up as he shoved his phone into his pocket. He adjusted his suit while walking to the door, and then took a moment before he unlocked it. Before Bing opened up, he rolled his head on his shoulders and pasted a friendly smile on his face. *Bastard.*

"What is it?" he asked as the face of her father's head of security, Raul, came into view.

He scanned the office as if looking for someone. "I thought I heard voices."

"That was me, talking to myself. There is nothing to be concerned about. You can return to your post," Bing assured while angling his body away from Raul.

With one final look around, Raul nodded and stepped out of the office. Well, at least she knew the head of security wasn't involved in Bing's plotting. That knowledge would come in handy when she made her move.

Over the next two hours, Giselle watched as Bing moved around her father's temporary office, not reviewing the pages left on the desk as he'd promised, which wasn't a huge surprise. His arrogance would be his downfall. She had to come up with a plan, and she'd need to enlist her bodyguards' help if she had any hope of stopping Bing and those he worked with. She prayed Shaw and Spence believed her.

This wasn't going to be easy.

But she'd learned: the most important things weren't.

CHAPTER NINE

Shaw

"You've got to look at this," Spence said as he brought over his laptop and set it in front of Shaw. It was only six in the morning, but neither of them had slept much. Spence had been busy with research, and Shaw had spent a good part of the night trying to figure out his place in his ever-changing reality.

He sat up and scanned the magnified image on the screen. It didn't take him long to find the person Spence was concerned about. A younger Bing stood in a crowd of people carrying a sign.

"When and where was this taken?"

"Moroso. November twenty-sixteen during an anti-government march outside the capital of Squr."

"Anti-government?" Shaw asked. "And now he's the assistant to the ambassador?"

"Riiight."

"What do these protestors want from their leaders?" Shaw asked. For all he knew, the Maas family might be tyrants.

"Contrary to the world waking up to climate change issues, and exploiting resources, this group was protesting the government's unwillingness to bulldoze through the country's resources."

"What?"

"The Maas family has taken a measured approach with its oil production. Instead of building more oil rigs and stripping the land, they've fought to preserve the natural balance."

"The people of Moroso want to produce more oil? Are they a struggling nation?"

"No. They have a good standard of living, and many services, such as hospitals, are free to all citizens. But there's a faction of unknown size pushing to increase yields and flood the market. Its leader is standing next to Bing. His name is Joven Cruth."

"That'll bring prices down. They'd end up losing money."

"Exactly. Which makes no sense unless there are forces who want to destabilize the country and overthrow its government," Spence stated.

"Shit. I bet that's exactly what they want to do," Shaw said as his mind raced. What the hell had they gotten themselves into?

"Overthrow the government?" Spence asked. "There goes our walk-in-the-park easy assignment."

"We knew something was sideways with that Bing dude. Now everything is coming clear. Bing's Joven's man on the inside."

"What the hell do we do with this? All I have is a picture and supposition."

"Call Brick." He was their team leader for a reason, and he had connections in places Shaw and Spence couldn't and didn't go.

There was a knock on their door, and Shaw shut the laptop. Spence went to answer it and found Raul on the other side.

"Giselle wishes to visit Santa Monica Pier today. She will be leaving at eight," he said before turning away and heading down the hallway.

"You'd better make that call. We need to get the ball rolling. I have a feeling time is not on our side." Shaw didn't even try to hide his frustration. "Shit. Last thing I expected was for this to go sideways."

"You and me both, buddy."

Three hours later, Shaw found himself on a Ferris wheel hovering above the Pacific Ocean while Spence watched from the boardwalk below. It was a sunny California day, and if circumstances were different, he'd kill to be out surfing, but that wasn't happening.

They'd contacted Brick, and he was reaching out to whoever while they were told to hang back and observe Bing, which was difficult given his current position.

"What would you say if I told you I wish to hire your team?" Giselle asked out of the blue.

"My team?" *What?*

"Yes. You and your friends who retired from the Navy. LH Investigations."

"What exactly would you need to hire us to do?"

Giselle took a deep breath as if stealing herself and said, "To protect my father from his assistant."

Stunned silent, Shaw looked at the young woman, who stared straight ahead as they rounded the top of the wheel.

"I've taken the time to research you and your friends, and I've found you are what I require."

"What makes you think Bing is a danger to your father?" Shaw asked, pissed he didn't have a connected com to Spence. Shaw knew better than to believe in coincidences and wondered if Giselle was fronting for Bing or if she was truly concerned for her father.

"I've heard him on a call discussing using my father as a means to end the Maas rule of Moroso. I don't know exactly what he's planning, and that's where you come in."

Bing had always been super careful when anyone was around. "How'd you hear this?"

"I've bugged my father's office."

Shaw wanted to be shocked, but he wasn't. "Of course you did. What's with the act every time Bing is around?"

"Can you think of any better way to keep your enemies clueless than pretending to be a spoiled child who is only concerned with herself?"

Huh. Smarter than they thought. "How long have you been suspicious of Bing?"

"About six months ago, I noticed he had two cell phones. They are close in appearance, but the new one has an extra port on the bottom, shaped like a circle. There's also my mother's gift that tells me something is seriously wrong with that man."

"Your mother's gift?" He hadn't seen a woman around the suites.

"My mother used to help advise my father about a person's character. She had a gift, they tell me."

"Tell you?"

"Yes. My mother died while giving birth to me."

"I'm sorry."

The young woman finally turned to face him. "Thank you. I refuse to lose another parent."

Shaw suspected Bing of something, and he'd been around the guy only a couple of days. Losing your only parent was a great motivator for Giselle to keep her eyes and ears open around her father. And she was no stranger to the inner workings of her country's government. His gut told him she knew what she was talking about. "We better get off this thing. Now."

"Agreed."

Shaw couldn't contain his curiosity about her ability to "see" people and figured, what the fuck, he'd ask. "What do you see when you look at me and Spence?"

"You and your friend have issues, but your characters aren't one of them. You can be trusted to do the honorable thing."

"Issues?"

"You carry a great amount of conflict within yourself, making it hard for you to see the natural path."

"Huh." He wasn't going to tell this kid she'd summed up the story of his life, wandering around in the dark when it came to forming anything resembling a relationship.

"You should let in the light," she said, as if reading his thoughts.

When the operator opened their buggy's door, Spence scanned the area as they approached him.

When he was a foot away, Shaw leaned in and said, "Brother, we need to talk."

CHAPTER TEN

Kyle

"Are you sure you don't want another piece of corn?" Alejandra asked as she held out a piping-hot platter of the spiced, cheesy goodness.

"I've eaten four already, but thank you for another lovely lunch."

Kyle had gone to visit the women who'd taken up residence in Roman's father's mansion at the end of the peninsula where Kyle now lived. He tried to visit as often as he was able to check on how they all were doing after being freed from their forced servitude.

Many months ago, he'd discovered Alejandra hiding behind his father's garage. That clandestine meeting led to uncovering a human trafficking ring, his parents' involvement, and his subsequent injuries. But he wouldn't change a thing about meeting her. If he hadn't, the rest of the women taking refuge in this house would still be in danger, or dead.

The decision to become their benefactor was an easy one. He had more money than he could spend in one lifetime, and these people needed his help. He'd arranged for tutors, language coaches, and lawyers to protect their interests. With any luck, the girls would be attending online classes in the fall. However, today, he was here for an entirely different reason.

As he watched the women bustling around the large kitchen, he was certain about his proposal. The mansion always smelled as if a feast was being prepared, and he never left his visits hungry.

"How are the classes turning out?" he asked Crystal, one of the two older ladies who worked to protect the vulnerable in Seattle, from where they'd all come.

"Most of the girls are picking up English quickly, which is encouraging, and they're settling in well."

"Is there anything you can think of you need, or something that might help with the transition?" If she said yes, he'd try to find it.

"You've already done so much."

"Not nearly as much as these women deserve."

"I have a small list I've been keeping when things pop up," she admitted before digging out the piece of folded paper from her apron pocket. "It isn't too much."

Kyle took the list and gave it a quick read before shoving it into his pocket. He'd make sure the items were ordered.

"How about the grocery site I signed you up for? How's it working out?"

"Exactly as you'd had hoped. The women look through it and add what they want to the monthly order. Spices, fresh food, meats, all the necessities. They often plan meals together months in advance. It's a luxury they've never known."

Looking around at the smiling faces, laughter, and camaraderie reminded him of the team who'd saved him. Which made him wonder, what was Shaw doing right now? It'd been a week since he left, and what had been an expected quick return had been extended with no end in sight.

Kyle pulled himself out of obsessing about Shaw and Spence's safety before his mood soured.

"I'm happy it's working out. There's another reason I came down to visit. I was hoping to speak to all the ladies."

Crystal's smile never wavered. "Alejandra, would you please gather everyone for a meeting in the living room."

"Yes, ma'am," she said and quickly rushed off.

Kyle turned his wheelchair and headed for the other room. Ramps had been installed so he could get around without too much effort. There was an elevator in the mansion that'd been installed when it was built. He assumed it was there due to laziness, considering no one who lived here had a disability. If he had the use of his legs, he'd run up and down the stairs every day.

The women began joining him and Crystal, and Kyle didn't miss several looks of concern pass between them. It would take a lot more time for them to accept they were safe after what they'd been put through. While what he'd experienced was nothing compared to what they had endured, he empathized with them: most nights he didn't sleep for more than a couple of hours.

"That's everyone," Alejandra said.

Crystal translated contemporaneously when Kyle spoke. "I have an idea that's been growing stronger, and I wish to share it with you." A few women nodded. "After enjoying the fabulous meals you've created, I believe there's an opportunity here for something special."

"Opportunity?" a girl named Marie asked. "That's what they said to get me on that truck from Mexico. What sort of opportunity?"

Kyle winced. What these women had experienced would never go away. Fade perhaps, but in the back of their minds, they'd always be suspicious. "Sorry. Poor choice of words. What I'm proposing is a business venture." More women looked trepidatious. He had to up his game. "Your food... I've never eaten so well in my life. Every time, without fail, you ladies put out Michelin Star quality dishes. I believe people would pay for your homemade sauces, dips, and more. We'd start small. Manufacture only a couple items, get a good distributor, and then we'll see where it goes."

"You want to make money off our family recipes?" a small voice in the back asked. He couldn't tell who had spoken.

"No. I want *you* to make money off your family recipes. Each of you would be part-owner in the company. *You'll* be responsible for the production and distribution after we've put everything in place and set up your online store. It's not going to be easy, but you can build your own nest eggs for the future and be secure *when* the company takes off. You'll have to work together, but you'd be your own bosses." The women looked from one to the other, trying to gauge their reactions. He knew it was a lot to drop on them, and they were probably waiting for the catch. "It will be written down and legal. I want to help you get started, but the profits would be yours. You don't have to decide right now. Talk it over, and we can revisit it if, or when you're ready."

Independence was what he wanted to give them, but they had to decide to take the chance. He never wanted to see any of them in a subservient role ever again. For obvious reasons, he felt protective about the group of twelve women. He was deeply invested in their lives, their future, and their success.

He hoped they took the chance.

CHAPTER ELEVEN

Shaw

Shaw looked at his phone and read the message for a second time.

Kyle: Fletch and Brick dropped me off at Bryan's today and left for LA. Is there something you're not telling me?

If he told Kyle the truth, he'd worry himself sick. He'd been through a traumatic experience and didn't need to be drawn into another situation. But if Shaw lied, he'd be breaking faith with Kyle.

Bryan: You don't have to go into detail. All we want to know is if you're safe.

He had to respond.

Shaw: I'm safe. The job has taken a turn that requires more boots on the ground. Logistics. Nothing to worry about.

Kyle: Easy for you to say, you're like some super soldier.

Shaw: That's the Army. I was in the Navy.

Bryan: Fine. Some super SEAL. Either way, be careful. All's good back home.

Home. The word rattled around in his head. Was this what it felt like to have a home where people waited for your return? He'd gone so many years without that it was hard for him to get a handle on the emotions that went along with the concept.

Shaw: You two ganging up on me from the same room?

Kyle: Maybe.

Shaw couldn't help but laugh.

Bryan: We just finished dinner and Grandad's eyeing the deck of cards. Looks like a game of poker might be in our future.

Shaw: Watch out for Kyle, the card shark.

Kyle: Hey, I can't help it if I'm good.

Shaw's mood had lifted as it always did when he communicated with these men.

Shaw: I'll leave you three to your game. Kyle, don't take all their money.

Kyle: We're only playing with pennies.

Bryan: Intentionally.

Shaw: Smart.

Kyle: 'Night.

Bryan: Good night.

Shaw stared at his phone long after the other two had signed off. He wasn't oblivious to the bond the three of them were creating. What that bond meant was the question of the century.

"Hey, lover boy, everything good at the ranch?" Spence asked from behind his laptop.

"Yeah. They're all good."

Spence stopped what he was doing. "They?"

Shit. "I meant Bryan. Kyle's staying over at the ranch since we're all out of town."

"Ahh, that's what you meant. For a guy not interested in commitment, you're building quite the little family."

"Family? What family?"

"Bryan and Kyle. Don't get me wrong. There's nothing wrong with a triad relationship. They happen all the time."

"Triad? There's no triad. There's barely even a couple."

"Keep telling yourself that." Spence smirked.

Shaw didn't want to discuss this with Spence or anyone. Especially not himself. "Go to sleep and take your fantasies to dreamland with you."

"I have a few more hours of research to get in, but you go ahead. I'll get more information out of you while you're talking in your sleep anyway."

"I don't talk in my sleep," Shaw grumbled as he rolled over to face the wall.

"Right. And nothing's going on between the three of you."

"Leave it alone, man."

"Fine, but when you need someone to talk to, I'm available."

"I'll keep that in mind."

***

Shaw almost laughed out loud when Brick and Fletch walked by hand in hand and set their blanket down a few feet away from where they'd set up Giselle with her luxe picnic. They were in Beverly Gardens Park off Santa Monica Boulevard under the guise of Giselle wanting fresh air and grass. As planned, to keep up her ruse, she threw a fit when Bing was hovering while she was in the rose garden.

Shaw and Spence were in jeans, button-down shirts, and jackets, trying not to look like Navy SEALs during an op. The boss and Fletch looked like they just jumped off a pride parade float, which in this neighborhood meant they blended in.

Fletch's shorts came straight out of the seventies, and Shaw was surprised his friend hadn't blown a ball by now. The fishnet muscle shirt Brick had on looked like it was digging into his skin. Their blanket was a giant rainbow, and the wicker picnic basket decorated in multicolored bows contained a new member of the team.

"Where the hell did you guys get a dog?" Shaw asked but made sure to look like he was talking to Giselle instead.

The little brown chihuahua even had a pink tutu. No one would suspect these two of anything but what they appeared to be: a couple having a picnic. They sat down with a flurry of touches, making it clear they were lovers.

"You can rent them," Brick answered while facing Fletch and pulling a bottle of champagne from a designer tote. "You can rent anything in LA."

Two glasses followed, and with a pop of the cork, they poured themselves drinks, and Fletch went ahead and laid his head on Brick's shoulder.

Shaw couldn't help himself: he slid his cell from his pocket and snapped a few pics. When would he ever have a chance like this again?

"Giselle, let's get this ball rolling," Spence said as he set the frisbee on her blanket.

Under the frisbee, she found dog treats. "Are these the ones the little darling likes?"

"Owner said she's crazy for them, time to test that out," Fletch whispered as if sharing a special moment with Brick.

Giselle carefully removed one of the treats and placed it beside her knee. The dog's head popped up so fast she looked like a bobblehead. She had the scent and was making her way over to Giselle.

Sure, enough the dog gobbled up the treat, and Giselle acted the part of surprised teenager. "Oh, my goodness, aren't you precious," she squealed as the animal licked its lips.

Brick and Fletch turned and played apologetic dog owners. "I'm so sorry. Is she bothering you?"

As they neared, Shaw and Spence blocked their way as they were expected to do as her bodyguards.

"Stand down, you two," Giselle ordered as if frustrated by their behavior. "Let them through." They backed away a few feet, and introductions began.

Spence picked up the dog and handed it to Brick, and in a soft voice said, "Giselle, meet Brick, the boss, and Fletcher, our teammate. They'll be laying low in case you see them when we're out and about."

Brick took the dog and said, "We wanted to meet so you have a chance to get a look at us. If you can't get to Shaw or Spence and something happens, come to one of us. We'll protect you."

"But I want you to protect my father, not me."

"You're a package deal," Fletch stated. "We have eyes on the ambassador as we speak."

With the four of them there, Shaw had to wonder who else was out there. "Who's the fifth?"

"Gunner agreed to help us," Brick advised. "He's infiltrated the staff charged with taking care of your suite. You should see him in passing, so make sure to point him out to Giselle."

"Yes, sir." It was so easy to fall back into their respected ranks when out in the field, and it made things run smoothly. "Do you have any more information?" There hadn't been much action on the spy-cam Giselle had hidden in her father's office.

Fletch lifted the dog into the air and made little kissy noises at it while Brick wrapped his arm around his shoulder. Proud puppy parents, like an effin' poster.

"There's a whole hell of a lot of moving parts with this, but we're concentrating on the ambassador's and Giselle's safety. I've been in touch with a few contacts I have in Moroso."

"Wait, you have contacts in Moroso?" Giselle gasped.

Brick smiled wide and took the dog from Fletcher before saying, "A life spent fighting one war after another comes with a few perks." He grinned. "Joven Cruth has gone underground, and his followers are regrouping. We're trying to find out why, unless he's planning to pop up like the country's savior once the Maas name is destroyed. As for Bing, he's no more than Joven's puppet. It's rumored the two are lovers, and Bing thinks he's more to Joven than a lay. We'll be in touch when we find out more."

Brick wrapped his arm around Fletch, and they said their good-byes as if meeting by chance as they returned to their blanket. Spence and Shaw packed up Giselle and their picnic stuff, then headed back to the hotel as if it they'd spent another typical day of sightseeing. Her driver was still an unknown, so they kept to the script while around him.

Shaw found himself excited to see his teammate again. Gunner was a fierce SEAL who hadn't retired when the four of them did, but here he was, part of the team again. Shaw wondered what'd happened after they left to make Gunner leave teams.

There'd be plenty of time to catch up after they prevented a possible coup.

CHAPTER TWELVE

Kyle

Kyle tried to remove the blindfold, but his arms were tied behind his back. Using his shoulder wasn't helping. He could hear water splash nearby, but he still had no clue where he was or if it was day or night. He'd lost all sense of time long ago, before they'd moved him to this new location.

His legs burned as if they were on a grill. The repeated beatings had rendered them useless, even though the pain was front and center in his mind. He was thirsty, and had been thirsty for so long he couldn't remember the last time he'd had a drink of water.

Every squeak had him jumping. He thought he was alone, but he wasn't sure if someone was sitting silently in the room with him. Given his sensory deprivation, he had no way of knowing. Everything was a mess, and the people he'd thought were his parents had turned into bloodthirsty murderers. How could he have been so blind to what was happening around him?

He was their prisoner until he told them what they wanted to know: where he'd hid all the proof damning them and all their friends. Like he believed that. The only way he was getting out of here was in a body bag, unless his brother found him first. Fletcher would find him.

The slow thud of footsteps approaching his door had him curling into himself. His pulse raced, and he couldn't stop the shaking that followed. They were coming back to try again, but he'd die before leading them to the women in hiding.

The doorknob squeaked as it turned, sending a chill down his spine. He knew what came next and did his best to appear knocked out, hoping they'd go away. He let his head hang down, and his body went lax, and he slowed his breathing to a whisper.

He heard the light switch click but didn't move a muscle. The footsteps stopped directly in front of him, freaking him the hell out. Moments later, his head flew back from the force of the blow to his jaw. He couldn't help but groan even though he'd refused to give them the satisfaction of his screams long ago.

"Have I got your attention?" His father's voice slurred from somewhere to his left. "Are you ready to tell me what I want to know, or do I carry on with my type of persuasion?"

The snap of the riding crop was a clear warning. Kyle remained silent. Fuck you, psycho.

He heard the slight whistle of air before the sharp leather tore into his already damaged legs. The pain was swift and felt like broken glass ripping through his veins. His father's sick laugh followed as it always did, a reminder of his insanity.

"You were always the good son. Look at you now. You're a disgrace to the Daniels name. I figured you of all my children would understand a good business deal when you saw it."

Another blow raked across his right knee, making his ears ring as the bastard did the same to his left kneecap. His stomach roiled, and nausea had him gagging without results since he hadn't eaten anything in weeks.

"Tell me, and all this stops." The smell of bourbon wafted from his father's breath, meaning his mother more than likely drove them here and was listening. How could anyone who gave birth to a child allow that child to be hurt?

Kyle thought about it and realized there was something he wanted to say before they went another round.

His dry, cracked lips ached as he tried to wet them with his tongue. It was no use.

"Water..."

"Are you going to talk?"

Kyle nodded, and his jaw screamed out in pain at the move.

"Here," his father said, and Kyle felt the edge of a glass being pressed against his lips. He didn't care what it was. He was dehydrated and needed liquid. Thankfully it was water. He took a couple of large gulps before the glass was pulled away.

"That's enough, start talking," he growled. "I knew you'd give in. You're weak."

Kyle couldn't help the small smile that curved his lips before he said, "I hope I'm around to see your pathetic ass in prison, you scum-sucking bastard."

The next blow landed across his shoulders before the psycho refocused on Kyle's legs. The burning pain shot through him like ever-growing waves of fire, and he was having a harder time catching his breath this time around.

He fought to free himself from the ropes holding him in place, but to no avail as the strikes were now coming in rapid succession. He had to hold on. He couldn't allow his parents to win, but the pain was all-encompassing as flesh was torn from the bone. He cried for help, knowing no one was coming, and waited for death to take him. Suddenly everything stopped, and he could hear his name being called. He struggled toward the voice. He knew that voice.

"Kyle. Wake up." Bryan's voice sounded closer. "You're having a nightmare. Wake up, sweetheart."

His eyes flew open, and he found himself being held in the handsome cowboy's arms. This was new, but not unwelcomed.

"Kyle, are you with me?"

"Yeah. Yeah. I'm awake," he gasped.

"Thank god. You had me scared with all the hollering for help. Are you okay?" Bryan's tone rang with concern.

Kyle scanned the room to find Isaiah sitting in his wheelchair in the open doorway. Shit. Kyle had woken everyone in the house with his uncontrollable screaming. He felt like an idiot. It'd been months and he couldn't shake getting lost in the terror still gripping his mind.

"I'm sorry I woke you. It was a nightmare, I guess. I'll try to control them better." Even if he had to stay awake all night.

"A doozy by the sounds of it," Isaiah said. "Now that everything's okay, I'll leave you two to it."

"Thanks, Grandad. Good night," Bryan said as Isaiah turned and rolled down the hallway.

Kyle was staying in the spare bedroom next to Isaiah's room while Bryan's bedroom was on the other side of the house. Kyle must've been yelling up a storm to get Bryan's attention from so far away.

"I'm sorry, really. I wish I could stop them." Now that his fear was abating, embarrassment came flooding in.

"No need. How often does this happen?" Bryan asked.

"Pretty much every night." No sense in lying. Since he'd be here for at least a couple of days, they'd soon find out on their own.

"How do you get any sleep?"

"I make do with what I get." Some days were better than others, and some days were hell.

"Not tonight, you don't," Bryan said as he released Kyle and shifted until he was leaning back against the headboard, his body stretched out over the covers. He was wearing a pair of loose gym shorts. "Okay, here's the plan. I'm going to stay by your side, and I'll watch over you when you sleep. If I get any sense you're having a nightmare, I'll pull you close so you know you're not alone. That way, maybe you'll be able to fall back asleep right away."

"Really?" Kyle asked. Shaw had done the same thing when Kyle first came out of the hospital.

"Really," Bryan said as he opened his arms. "Lay your head down and try to get some decent rest."

Kyle rolled the upper half of his body onto his right side and adjusted his legs to match. "You're sure?"

"Positive," Bryan confirmed before patting his chest. "I might be a little hairy, but it should do the job."

Kyle lowered his head to Bryan's broad chest, nestling in his thick dark curls, and made himself comfortable. When he stopped moving, Bryan slid his arm around Kyle's shoulders.

"Now, sleep."

And, unbelievably, he did.

CHAPTER THIRTEEN

Shaw

Things were moving along at a hurried pace as they prepared for Senator Reynolds and his staff to arrive. Bing and Ambassador Maas worked in the office while the security and staff checked every last detail.

Shaw had seen Gunner in passing. He was working among the kitchen staff as a chef, and remembered the man being one hell of a cook. Gunner could easily pass for a chef. His food was that delicious.

Shaw, Spence, and Giselle were doing their best to go unnoticed, sitting out on the patio enjoying the sunny day. Two garden doors led to the patio, which spanned the living room and office. Of course, the office curtains were drawn, and the door was most likely locked. But they didn't need to be inside the office to know what was going on.

Giselle pulled out her phone and lounged back in her chair while Shaw and Spence stood a few feet behind her, giving them a perfect view of the screen. The living room patio door opened, and Gunner walked out carrying a food tray.

While the door was still open, he said, "Miss Giselle, would you like to try one of the hors d'oeuvres I've created for the senator's visit?"

"Yes, please," Giselle said, having already been introduced to Gunner.

Once the door shut, the massive man continued forward and gently set the plate on the table beside Giselle.

"Man, I don't know if I can get used to you in that apron and paper hat knowing you could pick off a target over three thousand meters away," Spence joked while he appeared to be talking to Giselle.

"Laugh all you want, jackass, but these are delicious," Gunner replied while pointing at the tray.

Giselle made a move to indicate they should try the food if anyone were watching. Shaw picked up some delicate-looking thing in a puffed pastry that appeared ready to crumble at the slightest breeze, and ate it in one bite. Flavors he couldn't place burst across his tastebuds as the crunch of the pastry gave way to the savory cream inside.

"Holy shit, you made these?"

"Damn right." Gunner smiled. "Now, what do we know about the senator's visit?"

"He's here to sign a deal for a cooperative agreement and the drilling rights to one offshore rig we currently operate in the Red Sea," Giselle answered.

"Why would Moroso give away one of its wells?" Gunner asked.

"To foster relations with the American government. It's not a huge barrel producer, but it is a sign of our willingness to befriend the West."

"In essence, it's kiss-ass session," Shaw put it bluntly.

"Yes. That's what's supposed to happen," Giselle said without a hint of offense.

"I get the feeling there's more to this than a mutual agreement about fostering relations," Spence stated.

"Me too," Gunner said. "If things start shaking up, send me the signal, and I'll come running." He stepped back and dipped his head in a bow to Giselle before leaving out through the patio door.

"What's Bing planning?" Giselle growled.

"I don't know, but if it's going to happen, it's going to happen soon. You're expected to fly back home in two days," Shaw said.

They returned to their previous positions. Hiding their eyes behind dark sunglasses, they watched Bing and the ambassador moving around the office. Nothing looked out of place as Giselle's father read through a document before setting it down and leaning back in his chair as he said, "It's ready for signatures, and soon I hope to count the Americans as one of our allies."

"This is a bright new day for the people of Moroso, sir, and it was created by your hand. May peace rule for a thousand generations."

Shaw wanted to puke. The smarmy asshole played his part well, but they had to wait to see what his next move would be.

"I'll freshen up before our guests arrive," Ambassador Maas said as he stood and headed for the adjoining washroom.

"Yes, sir. They should be arriving soon."

The moment the door was shut, Bing undid the top button of his suit jacket and pulled out a new set of papers from under his shirt. Quickly, he replaced the one the ambassador had read with the new version.

"I think we have our answer," Spence said as he moved closer.

"He's changing what my father read to something I'm sure he shouldn't sign."

"Right. I'd bet my right hand those changes aren't good for your family or your people," Shaw said.

"Do you think the American senator is involved?" Giselle asked.

"It wouldn't be the first time a senator was bought off," Shaw stated.

Bing shoved the original version down his shirt, buttoned up his suit jacket, and straightened his tie. There was a knock on the door, and he opened it with a crack. Shaw couldn't see who it was, but as soon as the door shut, Bing announced, "Senator Reynolds and members of his staff are on their way up, sir."

The ambassador came back out of the washroom while drying his hands on a towel. "Good, good. If all goes well, I can spend the next two days with my daughter."

"I'm sure she will appreciate the time with you."

"Asshole," Giselle hissed. "What do we do?"

The next moment, there was another knock, and the office door opened, allowing Senator Reynolds and his two aides to walk in.

"Whatever it is, we gotta do it fast before anyone signs anything," Spence said. "I'll call in backup."

"Here's what we're going to do." Shaw leaned in, a plan formulating in his mind.

CHAPTER FOURTEEN

Bryan

Bryan watched Kyle and Missy circle the bur oak tree. Kyle's ability to direct Missy where he wanted her to go was improving by the day, and the joy on his face was unmistakable.

Bryan tried not to think about how comforting it felt holding Kyle last night. He'd had all kinds of guilt about the thoughts going through his head and his attraction to the man. Bryan and Shaw weren't exclusive or long-term, but it didn't mean Bryan wanted him any less. How could he want two men? There had to be something wrong with him.

"Looks like you're thinking pretty hard," Kyle said as he led Missy over to Bryan's side where he sat atop Ranger. "Everything okay?"

Bryan was quick to smile. "Great. You're getting the hang of riding Missy."

"Nice try." Kyle laughed. "What's on your mind?"

Bryan should've known he wouldn't be able to get away with deflecting. Kyle might be recovering from trauma, but the guy was smart as a whip. He'd built and sold companies, and had travelled the world. Pulling the wool wasn't going to work with him.

"You going to ask me to leave because I woke you guys with my nightmares?" The way he refused to look at Bryan gutted him.

"What? No. That's definitely *not* what I was thinking."

"It's okay if you do. I understand. Someone screaming in the dead of night isn't conducive to getting enough sleep to run a ranch."

"That's not it. If anything, it's the opposite."

"You want me to stay?" Kyle scrunched his brow.

Bryan hung his head and said, "I'm having inappropriate thoughts about you."

Kyle's eyes went wide. "Thoughts?"

"Not anything... Well, maybe a little. More like affection and attraction."

"For me?"

"Yeah."

"You sure?"

"I'm sure. Why wouldn't I be?" Kyle looked down at his legs. "I don't give a damn if you can walk. That doesn't make you any less amazing." They were going to have to work on his doubts.

Kyle's eyes got wide. "What about Shaw?"

"That's why I'm feeling so guilty."

"But we haven't done anything."

"It doesn't matter. I'm attracted to both of you. How messed up is that?" He waited for Kyle to ask to be returned to the lake house. Who wouldn't run for the hills after that confession?

Instead, Kyle nudged Missy forward until they were side by side and placed his hand on top of Bryan's. "Not as screwed up as you might think."

Bryan's head shot up, and he looked at Kyle, and saw the truth in his eyes.

Shit.

CHAPTER FIFTEEN

Shaw

"Help. Somebody, help," Giselle yelled loud enough to get the attention of everyone in the suite.

Shaw knelt over Spence, who was lying unconscious on the stone patio, or at least he appeared to be. Shaw pretended he was checking his teammate for a pulse as the doors to the living room and office flew open. Her father's security came running, as did the occupants of the office.

"What's wrong?" the ambassador asked.

"He collapsed and isn't waking up," Giselle replied while shoving at Spence's limp arm. "Please help him."

"Call for an ambulance," Ambassador Maas ordered. "Is he still breathing?"

"The paramedics have been called," Raul answered while running into the living room.

"His breathing is shallow," Shaw muttered. "And his pulse is weak."

"We were sitting out in the sun. Could it be sunstroke?" Giselle offered.

"Make way for the paramedics," Raul announced as he stepped onto the patio, followed by two men and a gurney. That was fast. Fletch, dressed in paramedics' garb, knelt beside Spence and began taking vital signs while Brick unloaded equipment from their bag.

With a glance over at the office, Fletch squeezed Spence's arm, giving him the signal to wake up. His eyes popped open.

"He's conscious," Brick announced as he knelt and placed an oxygen mask over Spence's mouth and nose. "That's a good sign. Let's load him up in the bus and get him over to Cedars-Sinai before he passes out again."

Shaw, Fletch, Brick, and Raul lifted Spence onto the gurney as Bing, the ambassador, and the senator watched. Once he was strapped in, they gathered their gear and began pushing the gurney through the living room patio doors.

"Now that that's over, we should return to the office to conclude our meeting." Bing directed with his arm out in the direction of the open door.

Ambassador Maas took Giselle in his arms and said, "I'm sure he will be fine, dear. They have excellent doctors in America. We will check in on him to make sure he's comfortable."

Seeing his concern for his daughter made Shaw even angrier at Bing's attempt to destroy the honorable man. From all he'd learned and seen, he had no doubt Ambassador Maas was one of the good guys trying to help his people.

Shaw followed the gurney out, along with Giselle, while the others returned to the office. However, instead of heading for the elevator, they took a sharp right and down the hall to an empty room. There were no guests on the floor except the ambassador, his staff, Giselle, and security. As soon as the door was shut, the fireworks began.

"I swear if your fears are unfounded, I'm going to lose your number," Raul growled, standing a few feet away from Brick.

"This is your contact?" Giselle said in obvious shock.

"Your father's head of security and I go back over twenty years," Brick replied then turned back to Raul. "This isn't a wild-goose chase."

Raul's security personnel didn't even bat an eye at the exchange. Most likely, they'd been given a heads-up beforehand. Spence sat up and removed his oxygen mask.

"I'll say it's not," Gunner said as he walked in with a covered tray in his hand. He removed the cover to reveal the contract he'd lifted from the office. "You might want to look at section seventeen of Bing's version of the contract they were about to sign."

Raul took the papers and turned to the page. At any moment, Shaw expected yelling to come from down the hallway when Bing discovered the bogus contract missing.

"That bastard," Raul growled. "He changed the wording to read not one oil rig out at sea but twenty-six rigs across the country. This would ruin us." That got the attention of everyone in the room.

"Who's the contractor named to do the work?" Shaw asked.

"SR and Associates Mining and Exploration," Raul stated.

"Samuel Reynolds. The senator has a lot of explaining to do," Brick said moments before everyone's head came up at the sound of a door crashing into the wall.

"I believe the show's about to begin," Shaw announced. "Have the authorities been called?"

"Yes," Raul answered before handing Giselle the phony contract. "You're the reason the people of Moroso are safe. I'll give you the honor." He bowed to her, as did the other members of the security force. "Your mother would be proud."

Giselle's eyes were big, but she nodded and took the contract.

"Where is security?" Bing yelled.

"We're on," Shaw grinned wide. He was looking forward to this.

Raul led his team down the hallway. While waiting for everyone to be directed back into the office, Shaw looked down at the young woman who'd saved her country.

"You ready?" he asked Giselle.

She took a deep breath and said, "Yes."

Giselle stood straight, her head high, the mantle of responsibility resting well on her shoulders. "No one will ever take advantage of my people." This was her time to show she was her parents' daughter.

She didn't bother knocking on the office door; she walked in, followed by Shaw, Spence, Brick, Fletch, and Gunner.

"What's the meaning of this?" Bing shouted as the room filled.

"Perhaps we should go," Senator Reynolds said as he attempted to stand.

Spence put his hand on the senator's shoulder, stopping him from getting up. "We wouldn't want you to miss all the fun, SR and Associates." The senator's face paled, and he sat back.

"Daughter, what is happening here?" Ambassador Maas asked as she drew closer to him.

"Father, I need you to trust me like you did my mother," she said while revealing the contract in her hands. Ambassador Maas looked down at the papers and then at Bing, standing a few feet away. With a nod, he sat down and allowed Giselle to carry on. "I'm sorry for not telling you of my suspicions long ago, but I had no proof." She held up the contract. "Now I do. Bing is working for Joven Cruth and has changed the terms in the contract to ruin the Maas name and remove us from power. He, along with Senator Reynolds, attempted to have you sign away twenty-six oil wells in our country to destroy our people."

Giselle opened the contract to the page where Bing had altered the terms and handed it to her father. "He replaced the one you reviewed when you left to wash up before the meeting."

"This is preposterous," Bing fired back. "I have always been a servant to you and the people of Moroso."

"Was that before or after you began your love affair with Joven?" Shaw asked, unable to remain silent when faced with this sad excuse of a man.

"They're making this up when they, themselves, switched the contracts. She's wild and selfish, wanting her freedom so badly that she's willing to destroy our country to get it," Bing growled as he took a step toward Giselle. Fletch cut off his route.

"How about you show them what's under your shirt and jacket," Brick said, daring Bing to continue. "I'm sure one of these fine security guards will help you with that."

As if on cue, a tall man in a suit came forward and patted the front of Bing's suit. "There is something underneath."

"How would you know all this? We were in the office alone," the ambassador asked.

Giselle didn't look away. "I planted a camera in your office to keep an eye on," she glared at Bing, "him."

The ambassador looked down at the papers in his hand then over to Senator Reynolds and Bing. "Take the traitors into custody and call the authorities."

Giselle smiled wide and ran into her father's arms. "Thank you for believing in me."

"You are your mother's daughter, and I couldn't be prouder."

Shaw saw Bing reaching into a guard's jacket and taking out his gun. He pointed it at the ambassador and Giselle, and Shaw reacted according to his training, and the only way he could by throwing himself in front of the pair.

The impact took his breath away, and the last thing he remembered thinking was it was a good thing Bryan and Kyle found each other.

CHAPTER SIXTEEN

Kyle

Kyle sat in his chair looking out the window at the twinkling Los Angeles skyline. At three in the morning, bar sign lights danced along the street, and people were still out enjoying the evening. Did anyone sleep around here?

He hadn't slept in days since receiving the phone call from his brother. Shaw had been shot protecting the ambassador and his daughter from the crazy-ass assistant who planned to bring down the Moroso government for a man named Joven Cruth.

The story was all over the news. A senator was under investigation, and there was talk of some citation or medal for Shaw's bravery. But all Kyle wanted was to have Shaw wake up for more than a few seconds at a time. The bullet entered his body below his vest, hitting his liver, which required major vein repair.

Every fear Kyle had felt when he was in the hospital came rushing back a hundredfold, but he had to keep it together for Shaw. When he did fully wake up, he'd need their help and strength as Kyle had when he was in hospital for months on end.

Bryan sat on the couch along the back wall staring at the same page in a book for over an hour. Both refused to leave Shaw to go back to the house the team had rented, preferring to remain by his side.

Whatever the hell was going on between the three of them was certainly more than friendship. Kyle and Bryan agreed, the need to care for Shaw would be priority. Then, maybe, they'd address what they meant to each other.

The team had been in and out all day, bringing in food and news. While they were attentive and concerned, they didn't seem to be worried about Shaw's recovery. Each of them made comments like, "He's had worse," "He's tough," "He'll be annoying the fuck out of us asking him to bring him shit."

Kyle knew the SEALs were trained within an inch of their life, but still. He wished he could be so cavalier. "He's going to be fine," he said out loud, wanting to hear the words.

"Yeah he is," Bryan said. He stood and walked to behind Kyle's wheelchair before laying his hands on Kyle's shoulders and squeezing.

He groaned as his tight neck and shoulder muscles cried out for relief. He always carried his stress in those spots, and today his muscles were hard as stone. Bryan got the hint and began rubbing and squeezing his tense body. It felt so good he allowed his head to hang down while Bryan's fingers did their work.

"Me next," Shaw's voice cracked when he spoke. Kyle and Bryan were by his side in a flash.

"How do you feel?"

"Is there anything you need?"

"I can call the nurse."

"Do you want a drink of water?"

Shaw smiled. "Good to see nothing's changed."

"You scared me," Kyle growled.

"Same here, and when we get you home, you better not think of running out into danger again. You take your time and heal while we take care of you," Bryan announced as if there wasn't another option.

"Yes, sir," Shaw said, his smile never faltering. "I knew you guys would be pissed."

"You promised it was an easy job," Kyle repeated what Shaw had told him before he left.

"No danger, you said," Bryan added.

"Things changed quickly. What's the doc say?"

"That you're on the road to recovery. The bullet nicked a vein in your liver. So far, there's no sign of complications."

"Good. When do we get out of here?" Shaw asked.

"You were shot less than two days ago, and you think they're going to let you out of the hospital?" Kyle asked, and here he thought it was him who hated hospitals the most out of this group.

"What can I say? I'm a fast healer. Besides, I'd rather be home on the ranch than here in LA."

"Agreed," Bryan said. "And as soon as the doctors give us the go-ahead, we'll bust you out of this place. Until then, rest and recuperate are the only two things you need to worry about."

"Got it," Shaw said, his voice already sounding sleepy. "With you two mother hens around, I gotta get outta here or I'm going to go stir-crazy."

Reaching out, Shaw took hold of Bryan's hand and then Kyle's. "Gotta say, it's nice to wake up to you two."

A few moments later he fell back to sleep. Kyle and Bryan sat holding Shaw's hands for a long time. As Bryan reached over and cupped Kyle's face, his vision blurred with tears.

"Don't worry. Everything's going to be fine."

***

Shaw

Shaw leaned back against the headboard as Kyle bounced around the bedroom like a honeybee. He'd fixed the flowers on the table by the window five times, closed the drapes for the night, and brought him another snack. The guy was running himself ragged while poor

Bryan was out the entire day moving the herd to fresh pastures to the east.

"Kyle, come here." Shaw had to stop him before he made himself sick.

He looked up and seemed confused, but came over just the same. "Do you need something?"

"Yeah. I want you to go and put on your sleeping pants and t-shirt for the night and come back here."

"Wh—"

"No. This isn't up for discussion."

"Okay," Kyle agreed though his confused expression remained.

Shaw had arrived at the ranch yesterday, and he was set up in Bryan's bedroom. He'd slept alone last night because his lover didn't want to jostle him in the night. Shaw didn't plan on a repeat of sleeping solo. The bed wasn't too high off the ground, so his idea should work.

He'd had plenty of time to think things through while laid up in the hospital. Bryan and Kyle hadn't left him by himself the entire time, but instead of feeling trapped and antsy, as he'd expected, he felt cared for and wanted. Two emotions at odds with what he typically tolerated: he'd never allowed himself to be put into this kind of situation before.

Kyle returned dressed as Shaw had asked. He held out his hand to Kyle, who'd been able to transfer from his chair to a bed for a while, and was getting good at it.

"Come on over here. It's time to rest."

"In bed with you? What if I hurt you accidentally?"

Shaw continued to hold out his hand and said nothing. Kyle would have to decide on his own if he wanted to get in bed with him. He couldn't help his smile when Kyle rolled up close to the bed and put on the hand brakes. Reaching up, Kyle took hold of the headboard while leaving one hand on the mattress.

Without a hitch, he transferred over and into Shaw's waiting arms. If he had any strength, he would've helped, but he was as weak as a baby, which he wouldn't tolerate any longer.

"This is much better," he said as he pulled the covers over Kyle and slid down to lay his head on his pillows. "'Night."

"Night, Shaw."

It took about five minutes for Kyle to begin snoring. The man was running himself ragged, when all Shaw wanted was this. He heard the back door open, and footsteps were headed their way. Bryan appeared in the open doorway and stood stock-still.

"Go have your shower, then get that gorgeous ass over here," Shaw said while pulling back the covers on his other side.

Bryan's smile was instant as he headed for the bathroom, and fifteen minutes later, he crawled into bed.

"How are you and Kyle?" Bryan asked. He'd left before dawn this morning.

"He was rolling around here like a tornado. I took matters into my own hands. Now that you've gotten back, it's about perfect. Go to sleep, and we'll talk in the morning."

Bryan leaned up for a kiss Shaw was happy to give. "Good night."

"'Night, Shaw," Bryan said as he laid his head down on his shoulder and reached over to touch Kyle's arm. "This isn't going to be easy."

"Best things never are."

CHAPTER SEVENTEEN

Bryan

Bryan left Shaw and Kyle in bed then went out to the barn early to get his chores done so he'd have a few moments with the guys later. He was on his second stall by the time his grandad showed up with a thermos of coffee.

"Coffee sounds great, thanks," Bryan said as he leaned the shovel against the wall of the stall and reached for the thermos.

"Thought you might be needing some with the hours you've been keeping."

"Hard work won't kill me," Bryan said as he unscrewed the cap and took a long inhale of the heavenly brew. "Yesss."

"Made it the way you like it."

"You want some, Grandad?"

"No, no. That's for you."

Instead of pouring himself a cup, he tilted the entire thermos back and drank directly from it. It tasted as good as it smelled, and warmth spread through his body.

"Oh yeah. That's the stuff," he said while resealing the top to keep the liquid warm.

When he looked over at his grandad, he saw Isaiah had one of those *we're about to have a talk* looks on his face. "Spit it out," he said. "What's got you worked up?"

"You have to ask?"

No, he didn't, but he wanted his grandad to start the conversation.

With a shrug of his shoulders, his grandad said, "It's about you, the SEAL, and the businessman."

"Walked into the bar, and the cowboy said," he teased, but Grandad didn't bite. "Okay, what about us?" Bryan had been waiting for this moment. The first time someone asked what was going on between the three of them, and the someone was his grandad. The person he loved most in this world, respected, and honored.

"I'm worried for you."

That wasn't what he'd expected.

"Worried? Why? I'm fine."

"A relationship is tricky enough without throwing in a commitment-phobe, as well as a man less than a year out of a traumatic life event. It ain't no solid combination, son."

"You're worried I'm going to get my heart broken?"

"Yep. Now I know both boys are good men. That's not part of the concern. What if Shaw realizes he doesn't want to be attached to two men? Or if Kyle decides he doesn't want to stay here in Texas long-term? Where does that leave you?"

"Let me get this straight. Your concern has nothing to do with it being three people and not two."

"Son, I don't give a rat's ass how many people you love, just as long as they love you back and don't leave you high and dry in the end."

Bryan couldn't help himself. He bent and gave his grandad a long hug. "Thank you."

Grandad's eyes looked a little glassy. "Thank me for what?"

"Understanding. I know both of those things you mentioned could be a reality, but I choose to enjoy every moment that we have together until then. The future isn't guaranteed. You and I know that best of all."

Bryan couldn't help but think of his parents anytime the subject of his future came up. They'd had so many hopes and dreams before their lives were cut short by some random accident. Random. You couldn't prepare for that hell. His mom, dad, and grandad were on their way back from a livestock auction over in Laredo when a drunk driver crossed the center line and hit their truck and trailer head-on.

They hadn't wanted Bryan to miss school, so he'd stayed home with his grandmother. He was nine, and he could still hear his grandma crying out hysterically when she got the phone call. His mom, who was pregnant, and his dad died at the scene. His grandad, who'd been asleep in the backseat of the truck, was crushed, which resulted in him being paralyzed.

The joys of boyhood ended for him that day.

"Yep, you're right," Grandad agreed. "But living in the moment and not planning ahead isn't the answer."

"What is?"

Grandad threw his hands in the air. "Damned if I know."

A few of his ranch hands came walking in to start their day. "You and Isaiah out here at it early this morning, boss."

Bryan was fortunate to have a loyal group of men helping him manage the ranch. No one could run an operation this big without help. A few lived on the property in a cabin behind the barns.

"I slept so well I woke up raring to go," he replied with a laugh. Remarkably, what he told them was true.

The time for talking over, Grandad backed out of the stall.

"Thank you," Bryan said. "I love you and promise to be careful."

"Love you too. If you need me, you know where to find me."

That he did, and Bryan was happy to have him by his side.

***

Kyle

Kyle's eyes opened and realized he wasn't in the spare bedroom. He'd been exhausted last night and thought he might've imagined the whole sharing Shaw and Bryan's bed. Considering the warm body by his side and the sunlight streaming in from the crack in the drapes, there was nothing imaginary about it. He was shocked. He hadn't woken up once with a nightmare.

"'Morning. You slept well," Shaw said, confirming what Kyle thought.

He leaned up on his elbow and looked around the room. "'Morning. Did Bryan come in last night?"

"Yeah, but you were asleep. He was quiet when he crawled into bed."

"Okay, um… The three of us slept together?"

"Yeah."

Shaw's smiling face was reassuring, but Kyle needed to say one thing first and foremost. "I don't want to come between the two of you."

"You're not," Bryan said as he came walking through the bedroom door carrying three mugs of what smelled like coffee.

Kyle adjusted his legs and pushed himself up into a seated position while Bryan set the mugs down and rushed to put pillows between his back and the headboard.

"There you go," Bryan said before leaning down and giving Kyle a quick kiss. Really only a peck, but it might as well have been full tongue with how surprised he was Bryan had gone ahead and done that in front of Shaw.

Then Shaw leaned forward and kissed Kyle in much the same way before Shaw and Bryan kissed and handed out the coffees.

"Okay, I'm confused."

"What are you confused about?" Bryan asked.

"Have we turned into a throuple?"

"Throuple, that has a certain ring to it," Shaw stated.

Okay, he had to be still asleep and dreaming all this because wishes and fantasies don't come true unless you're in a fairy tale. And everyone would agree, his life was no stinking fairy tale. Kyle didn't care if he looked stupid. He reached over and pinched his arm anyway. *Ouch.*

"But you hate commitment. How's having two of us going to cure that?"

Shaw's expression turned serious. "Unless either of you intends for this to be an open relationship, as in you have other lovers, we should be fine."

Bryan looked as confused as Kyle felt. "Open?" he asked as he crawled into bed on Shaw's opposite side.

Shaw let out a deep breath. "I learned young not to trust the word 'commitment.' My parents were and still are polyamorous. Hell, the whole neighborhood where I grew up was like them. Married meant little to them, and bed swapping was a way of life. I heard all the reasoning in the world from my parents. It was fun, and everyone was a consenting adult. They never pushed their way of life on anyone. I was to keep my opinions to myself."

"But you were a child," Kyle's voice shook. "You didn't have a choice. You were forced to live in the same house as they carried on around you."

"It feels hypocritical for me to judge them now that we," Shaw said as he pointed between the three of them, "are contemplating a triad relationship."

"You are not a hypocrite. You were a child facing what you didn't understand. I'm all for live and let live, but I draw a very sharp line when it comes to children's emotional abuse," Bryan stated. "They didn't even try to shield you from their choices or be discreet when you were around. They were forcing the incomprehensible on you before you were even old enough to understand."

"We are nothing like them," Kyle added. "The three of us won't be jumping into other people's beds. There would be our bed for the three of us, and only us."

"I don't intend to share either of you," Shaw said, "with anyone outside the three of us."

"So we going to give this a try?" Kyle asked. "You both sure when it comes to me and my baggage?"

Bryan set his and Shaw's mugs down before taking Kyle's and doing the same. He reached over and carefully lifted and adjusted Kyle until he was positioned between Shaw and him.

"Let's clear this up once and for all," Shaw stated as he wrapped his arms around Kyle. "You're no burden. You're an amazing man who doesn't know the word 'quit.' You're stronger than many people I know, and most of those bastards are tough as nails."

"You're handsome and brave, with a heart of gold. Those women you rescued have a chance at a good life thanks to you," Bryan continued. "Who in their right minds wouldn't want you?"

Kyle couldn't stop his heart from racing. Could it be true? Was he still desirable? "Is it okay if we move things slowly until I can see what you both see?"

Both men smiled wide, and Bryan pulled him close. "We'll go as fast or slow as you want."

He leaned into the hold as the three of them shared this life-changing moment. Then Kyle remembered something critical.

"My brother's going to kill you."

Shaw chuckled deep in his chest. "Wouldn't be the first time someone tried."

"That's not funny," Bryan growled.

"What? Too soon?"

CHAPTER EIGHTEEN

Shaw

The team had been over several times in the past two weeks, and today they were throwing a barbeque to celebrate Shaw's clean bill of health. He wasn't able to return to missions yet, but he could walk without pain, and he was getting his strength back. He'd take the wins.

Kyle hadn't been ready to share their relationship status with his brother, which meant the team was still in the dark. Gunner had returned with them and was currently staying at the lake house with the others until he decided what he wanted to do. Shaw still hadn't had the opportunity to talk with his old friend much since the shooting. He still wondered what could have driven Gunner away from the SEALs after the team had retired.

"This is looking great," Brick said as he joined Shaw at the grill. "I'm glad you're recovering fast. It'd be hard to replace you." Brick's smile told him that the boss was joking, but he understood. Sometimes it was hard for men to express what they meant.

"Wouldn't want to leave you high and dry."

Both laughed as he flipped the steaks, making the flames shoot up as the meat sizzled.

"Hey, I've been meaning to ask you to give me a heads-up before telling Fletch, okay?" Brick asked, putting Shaw on alert.

"Tell Fletch what?" The moment the words were out of his mouth, he knew the boss wouldn't buy it.

"What the three of you have been hiding these past weeks." Brick raised a single eyebrow.

"I'm not sure what you're talking about."

"Sure you do. But I respect your privacy. I'm only asking for the warning so I can jump on the big guy's back to slow him down long enough for you to get away."

"Gee, thanks." He could walk without pain, but running might be another matter.

"The guys and I have a bet to see if he puts you back into the hospital." Brick chuckled.

"You're a true friend," Shaw growled.

"How's it going over here?" Spence asked as he joined them at the grill.

"Are you part of this bet?" Shaw asked.

"Of course." Spence nodded. "Stay out of the hospital, and I'll share a third of my winnings with you."

"Only a third?"

"Yeah, me, you, and Rick."

Hell.

Shaw looked across the back deck at Bryan and Kyle. Both smiled back at him, and the sick feeling that'd been creeping up on him disappeared. He couldn't think of any better reason to risk going back to the hospital than those two men.

"Here," he said as he handed over the metal tongs to Brick. "I've got somewhere I'd rather be."

Shaw made a beeline to his men, who were busy setting out salads, corn on the cob, and baked potatoes.

"How's the steak coming?" Kyle asked when he neared the table.

"Great, but we have to talk. The team knows."

"About us?" Bryan asked while looking around at the crowd gathered.

"Yeah. And they're waiting for Fletch to figure it out. I know you're hesitant to tell everyone, but I'd feel a whole lot better if we told him before that happens." He respected the big guy and refused to have him find out about their unconventional relationship that way.

Kyle's eyes were wide, but they soon refocused and he appeared determined. "You're right. I want to be the one to tell him."

"When?" Bryan asked.

"Now's a good a time as any," Kyle said.

"Maybe we should be closer to the house so Shaw has a chance to run inside and lock the door," Bryan suggested.

"That won't be necessary," Kyle stated as if it were fact.

Shaw wished he felt as sure, but there was no way in hell he was backing out. The last few weeks living with these men had been the happiest of his life, and he wouldn't hide that. If Fletch wanted to knock him on his ass, so be it.

Bryan and Kyle came around to the front of the tables, and Shaw joined them. Why did he feel like he was headed for the gallows?

"Can we have everyone's attention?" Bryan spoke up.

Shaw caught sight of Fletch and his boyfriend, Sheriff Elias Cooper, near the bar, along with Roman and Rick. Bryan stood to one side of Kyle while Shaw stood on the other. This was it. Let the chips fall as they may.

***

Kyle

Kyle felt exposed having the group staring at him like this, but he refused to curl up in fear. This was his life, and he would live the remainder of it the way it made him happy. Before the events that changed his life forever, Kyle was fixated on work, money, and success. However, his priorities now were more philanthropic, and his time better spent enjoying life instead of racing through it. They weren't hurting anyone with their union, and he would forever be grateful for the time Shaw and Bryan gave him to figure that out.

"Can we get a dog?" Kyle asked while looking up at his men. He'd never had a pet.

"You're asking that now?" Shaw asked as his eyebrows drew together.

"I've always wanted a lab or golden retriever," Bryan said.

"A big ball-of-love yellow lab sounds perfect," Kyle answered.

Shaw looked between them and smiled. "What the hell am I going to do with the two of you?"

"The two of them?" Fletcher asked from much closer than he'd been a few minutes ago. *Shit.*

"We're getting a dog," Kyle cheered, confusing his brother further.

"That's going to require a larger explanation," Fletcher said as he came to stand in front of the three of them, his arms crossed over his chest.

Kyle could feel Bryan shift slightly closer to Shaw. Undoubtedly, preparing to protect him, even though he was the biggest of the three of them. But Shaw hadn't fully recovered and couldn't take on Fletch without getting hurt.

Kyle spoke before either of his men had a chance to say a word. "You know, four legs, wagging tail, covered in fur."

"I don't mean about the dog, and you know it. Why would the three of you be getting anything together?" Fletcher asked as he handed his bottle of Lone Star to Sheriff Cooper.

Isaiah moved his electric wheelchair closer as if sensing the change in mood.

"Man, you don't make things easy," Kyle said, followed by a loud huff. "Yeah, the three of us. We three. Trio. Triad. Throuple. Whatever you want to call it. I've been sitting around worrying about what you'd say or do when you found out. Recently, I discovered I don't give a shit."

"You guys are in a romantic relationship?" Fletch asked. "All three of you?"

"Yeah, and we're happy." Kyle smiled wide. "Thanks for asking."

Fletcher looked up at Shaw, his face stone cold. "You told me you wouldn't inflict yourself on my brother. Exact words." Yup. Fletch didn't look happy. "You lied to me."

"No. I didn't lie. When we talked, I had no intention of doing anything about my attraction to Kyle." Shaw moved his hand to Kyle's left shoulder.

"Then how did we end up here?" Fletcher growled and stepped closer, causing the entire team to set down their drinks.

"That would be on me," Bryan said while moving his hand onto Kyle's shoulder as well. "I realized I was attracted to both Shaw and Kyle."

"I remember the guilt you had admitting that because in your mind you were cheating on Shaw by having those thoughts," Kyle said. "Then Shaw was shot, and it expedited us admitting that we wanted to be together."

"Look, it's not Bryan I have concerns over," Fletcher said. "Shaw doesn't do commitment. He can't change his stripes."

"Hell, man, look at us. We've all changed since getting out. Brick's in a relationship with the son of a man who tried to steal his land. Spence doesn't have his face in a laptop twenty-four anymore, and even you have opened up and started talking way more than you ever did when you were on our team. It took these men to show me commitment isn't a four-letter word, and for them it's worth giving it a try. I'm not going anywhere without these two."

"But—"

"No more talk about this," Kyle said and felt his voice getting steely. "I love you, brother, that will never change, but the ranch is my home now, and I'm living here with Shaw and Bryan. I'm happy."

Fletcher looked around at the assembled group. "None of you look surprised."

"It was plain as day, my man," Spence said, nodding at Rick by his side.

"He's going to hurt you and break your heart." Fletcher's tone had deepened, and the muscle in his jaw jumped.

"I'm a grown man who's able to make my own decisions. This chair doesn't change that or define me. I'm still a whole person whether I stand again or not. If the worst happens, and I get my heart broken, I'll deal with it as an adult no matter how unlikely it is," Kyle stated. "But don't worry, I'll let you beat them up if they do."

"Don't think I won't," Fletcher vowed as Elias wrapped his arms around him. There was no fight left in his brother. "Don't mess this up, you two idiots."

Shaw and Bryan nodded, and that seemed to signal the party to start back up. Money exchanged hands, and Spence came over and handed Shaw his cut. "Thanks for staying out of the hospital."

"Congratulations, you three," Roman said as he walked up and hugged each of them. "I'm so happy for all of you."

One after the other, the team came over to talk to them, and give their support. His brother was still grumbling, but Kyle didn't back down, and when it came to his men, he never would.

***

Shaw

Later that evening, Shaw was busy putting dishes into the dishwasher while Bryan and Kyle were getting ready for bed. They hadn't had sex together yet because this was Kyle's first gay relationship, and they figured they'd take it slow. Which he respected, but his dick was going to fall off with all the jacking off he was doing in the shower on the daily. Who could blame him, being sandwiched between Bryan and Kyle?

Once the last plate was loaded, he threw in the soap pod, shut the door, and turned it on. Shaw had to adjust his hardening cock while walking down the hall, knowing his men were waiting for him in bed. He had to get control of himself.

When he came closer to their bedroom, he could hear the shower running. When he entered, nobody was in bed, so he closed the doors and began stripping on his way to the bathroom, which was filled with steam. He found Kyle's empty wheelchair in front of the counter. They had retrofitted the bathroom to suit Kyle's needs, meaning he must be in the shower on his bench. Moans echoed through the space, and he stepped out of his jeans and boxer briefs.

The shower was big enough to fit six people, so they'd have more than enough room for the three of them. Shaw walked through the opening and was greeted by a sight that had him groaning. Bryan was down on his knees in front of Kyle, who was on his shower bench, sucking Kyle's cock down to the root.

"Fuck, you two are gorgeous," Shaw said, the rumble of his emotions coming through in his tone.

Kyle's face was a study in pleasure. His hooded eyes, flushed face, and swollen lips were an invitation to be kissed. One Shaw gladly accepted. He made his way farther into the shower and leaned down to kiss Kyle as he'd always wanted to. All need and tongue, desperate to explore each other fully.

The hot water sprayed over his body, further enveloping him. A tentative palm wrapped around his cock elicited another groan, but he didn't break the kiss. Instead, he flexed his hips in the same rhythm as his tongue sliding into Kyle's mouth. When they separated, the handsome man looked even sexier with his blond hair sticking up at odd angles from Shaw running his fingers through it.

He ran the palm of his hand down Bryan's back, following the trails of water from the rainfall showerhead above them. His lover's response was instantaneous as he arched his back and lifted his ass in invitation.

"How can I say no to that?" He chuckled while grabbing the waterproof lube and a condom from the shampoo rack.

He dropped the sealed condom package on the ground by Bryan's right knee before squeezing the lube onto his finger, leaning over his cowboy's broad back, and circling his hole. His lover's moan gave Kyle an unexpected throat massage as his dick was still buried in Bryan's mouth, making him cry out in pleasure.

"That's it, babe, suck him down," Shaw said before inserting his index finger into Bryan's tight ass, making him moan harder.

Kyle held on tight to his bench as Bryan doubled down on his efforts, and Shaw slid in a second finger. He leaned forward and took Kyle's lips in another kiss as his fingers were deep inside of Bryan, stretching him. They were all physically and emotionally connected, and nothing had ever felt so real.

Shaw ended the kiss and moved up behind Bryan. He quickly rolled on the condom and lined the head of his cock up with Bryan's hole. He kept his eyes glued on Kyle the entire time, holding their connection intact. As he slid in deeper, the intimacy of this moment seemed to surround them.

Kyle's eyes closed as Shaw bottomed out, and moments later, Kyle groaned his release into Bryan's mouth. A switch clicked inside of him, and as Bryan released Kyle's cock, Shaw wrapped his hands around Bryan's waist and upped his speed.

After several minutes he reached around, took his lover's cock in his hand, and pumped it along with his strokes. Bryan's moans were getting louder as Kyle held on to his shoulders. Shaw could feel his orgasm bearing down on him, but he refused to come before Bryan.

"Squeeze his nipples," he told Kyle. "Nice and hard."

Kyle looked at him, unsure. "Hard?"

"Yeah. He loves it."

There was no hesitation after that as Kyle reached for Bryan's nipples and squeezed. The results were immediate. Bryan cried out, and his cock throbbed in Shaw's hand as Bryan came, his ass clamping down on Shaw's cock until he was barely able to move. One, two more strokes, and he followed his lovers over the edge into bliss.

The three of them stayed in the shower, cuddling and exploring until their hands were all pruned up.

Hours later, Shaw lay in bed with his arms wrapped around his men.

If this was a dream, he never wanted to wake up.

CHAPTER NINETEEN

Bryan

Bryan kept Ranger at pace with Missy as he and Kyle rode across the pasturelands toward the property's eastern edge. Kyle's riding had improved substantially over the past couple of months; he was at a point where they could go farther, and for longer. It gave Bryan the chance to show him the true breadth of Double M Ranch.

The rolling hills and limestone outcroppings surrounded them, including oak trees and sumac shrubs. Wildflowers bloomed in patches throughout the grasslands, and in the distance, his herd of longhorns grazed peacefully. He lived and owned a piece of paradise and never forgot it.

They were getting close to one of the private backroads cutting through their land, and when they reached it, they agreed to turn back for home. This was the longest distance Kyle had gone, and he still had a peaceful smile on his face. Since that unforgettable night in the shower, the three men had set a frantic pace when it came to their lovemaking. It wasn't odd for him to wake up in the night and find Shaw with his dick in a moaning Kyle or being woken by lips and tongues exploring his body.

He often wondered how he'd gotten so lucky to have these men in his life. As with his land, their relationship was paradise, and he'd never take them for granted.

"Getting thirsty?" he asked as he reached for his canteen. The Texas sun was beating down without a cloud in sight.

"I could use a drink." Kyle brought Missy closer.

Bryan unscrewed the cap and handed the canteen over to one of the men he was falling in love with. They'd taken Kyle into town a few weeks back to get more ranch-appropriate wear: boots, jeans, and a white cowboy hat. Bryan had to admit Kyle made a sexy cowboy.

Shaw was back at the house trying his hand at repairing one of the ATVs that'd given up the ghost without hope of ever running again. Brick and Gunner were out of town on a job while the rest of the team repainted the lake house. Everything had returned to normal, and Bryan was thankful for the slower pace. It gave him time to appreciate his new life and enjoy their time together.

"Who's that?" Kyle asked, pointing off to his left.

Bryan turned to look where Kyle was pointing and saw a dark-colored four-door car pulled over on their private sideroad. Two individuals stood near the rear trunk area, and though he wasn't close enough to be sure, Bryan thought they might be using binoculars.

"I don't know," Bryan said. "I want you to stay here while I go check them out."

"I don't like the sound of that. How about we both go home?"

Before they could come to an agreement, the strangers climbed into their car and left. Weird. What the hell were they looking for?

"Can we go back to the house now?" Kyle asked, his voice shaking.

"What's wrong?" Bryan asked as he drew closer and took hold of Kyle's hand. His smile was gone, his expression fearful

"It's possible they're looking for me. I left a lot of pissed-off people back in Seattle."

Bryan began leading Kyle away from the road then pulled out his cell phone, and when Shaw picked up, he said, "We may have a problem."

***

Shaw

Shaw raced inside the house and grabbed his Glock from its locker. This wasn't happening. He had to get to his men even though Bryan had said the intruders had driven away. They could turn back. Shaw passed Isaiah on his way outside.

"What's going on?" Isaiah asked.

"We're safe, but call the lake house and get the team out here." He may be overreacting, but Kyle was responsible for the imprisonment of many rich and high-ranking officials. Revenge was a powerful motivator, and his lovers could be in danger.

He jumped onto one of the ATVs and headed in the direction they'd be riding in. The sooner he could confirm they were okay, the quicker he could go on the hunt to find the intruders.

With any luck, they'd discover it was someone who was lost, though his gut instincts didn't think it would be that easy. Who or what were they looking at through the binoculars? What did they want? Questions swirled as he drove on, keeping an eye on the horizon for any sign of Kyle and Bryan.

The thunder of hooves had him looking off to his right to find three of the ranch hands headed his way. Isaiah must have radioed them to help as they fell in line behind him. Bryan treated his workers well, and they were loyal. After several tense moments, he caught sight of his men in the distance riding straight for him.

Not wanting to spook Missy or Ranger, he slowed the ATV and came up to them at a gentler pace.

"Are you guys okay?" Shaw asked as he jumped off and approached them.

"Yeah," Bryan answered. "You brought the cavalry?"

"Thank your grandad for that."

"Isaiah radioed you needed help, boss," Joe, the lead ranch hand, said while the other three men spread out around them on horseback. Each was keeping their gazes on the horizon.

"We have trespassers running around with binoculars. I want you to keep an eye out, but don't approach them. Report it to one of us, and we'll take care of it. Also, I want each of you to carry a rifle with you," Bryan said.

"Who are they?" Joe asked.

"We aren't sure, but they took off when we noticed them. Never a good sign."

Shaw stood beside Kyle, who was noticeably upset, and rubbed his leg in an attempt to comfort him. "It's going to be okay."

Kyle nodded but didn't say a word.

"Let's get back to the house. We can figure it out there," Shaw stated, knowing Kyle felt exposed out there in the middle of the pasturelands.

"Agreed," Bryan seconded. "Let's get home."

Shaw got back on his machine and drove beside Missy while Bryan rode on the opposite side. Joe and the other two ranch hands maintained a circle around them, keeping a lookout. The joy he felt this morning at seeing his men ride out was long gone, now replaced with worry and an overwhelming need to protect what was his.

As they approached the barns, he could see Fletch's truck parked by the house and knew he'd probably driven there like a madman. Much the same as Shaw had done on his way out to find his men in the pasture. When they reached the barn, Shaw undid the straps holding Kyle onto his saddle and helped him off the horse. Instead of placing him in his wheelchair, Shaw carried him across the yard and into the house.

Kyle's silence was like a knife to Shaw's heart. To see the normally happy man withdraw into himself made Shaw angry. Those assholes in Seattle didn't know who they were dealing with.

***

The Bad Guys

"Did you see him?"

"Yes, sir. He's there."

"How many are on the ranch?"

"From what we've seen, three ranch hands, an old man in an electric wheelchair, and the other two you already know about."

He sat back in his seat as San Antonio's Westside Deco District flashed outside his window. "I'll be there soon. Don't do anything until I get there." He ended the call.

All he needed was for one of those buffoons messing with his plans. Revenge would be sweeter by his own hands. It was only a matter of time before he had the man responsible for his losing everything he'd worked years to create at his feet begging to die.

There'd be no peace or mercy shown. They were well past the time for a pardon. Now punishment must be doled out personally.

An example had to be made.

CHAPTER TWENTY

Kyle

Kyle hadn't been outside in days. The world didn't look as bright as it had less than a week ago. He missed Missy and their rides, but he especially missed the freedom he'd begun to feel. The normalcy he craved had been torn away once again.

At least his brother, Shaw, and Bryan were in agreement for once. The unfortunate part was that they all agreed he had to remain inside to be safe while they looked for the strangers. Sheriff Cooper and his deputies searched the county while Brick and Gunner joined in his protection detail.

There were hourly patrols of the ranch, and Spence had installed the mother of all security systems on the property. Sensors were in place all over the land. No one could sneak up on them. Hell, all he had to do was utter the word "alarm," and the security system went crazy. Bells and alarms sounded, lights flashed, and people came running.

He knew they were doing this to keep him safe, but Kyle was beginning to feel like a prisoner. He felt guilty thinking that way, considering the amount of effort the people involved in protecting him were putting in. It was a catch twenty-two. If he tried for more freedom, it would look like he was disregarding their attempts to keep him safe. If he said nothing and continued to sit in the house all day, every day, he was going to lose it.

"Hey, there you are," Shaw said as he walked into the living room where Kyle was trying to lose himself in a game show on TV.

"Where else would I be?" He hadn't intended it to sound so sarcastic, but he was frustrated. "I'm sorry. I shouldn't've said that."

Shaw came over and sat in the chair beside his wheelchair. He took hold of Kyle's hand and said, "I can understand your frustration. Let's hope this won't last too much longer."

"Then what? They send someone else to take me out?" He couldn't see how any of this was going to end well. "In the meantime, my presence is endangering all those around me. What if someone gets hurt or worse?" He was getting worked up. He could hear the blood pumping in his ears. The world felt like it was working against him. One moment he couldn't be happier, the next the walls came crumbling down. How fair was this to those around him? "My life is never going to be normal again. I see that now." He wished he could pace. He'd been a pacer and always found it helped him think. He looked over at Shaw, who hadn't said another word but sat staring at the ground. "Am I boring you?"

Instead of speaking, Shaw pointed down toward his right leg. Kyle grumbled in frustration, but turned to see what he was looking at. He gasped. His right leg was no longer limply held by his foot in the footrest. It was flexed outward, and his foot was placed flush on the ground as if he were trying to get up.

"Did I move that?" It couldn't be, could it?

"You moved your right leg," Shaw said with all the amazement of a child opening presents. "You moved it. I saw it lift and move forward." Kyle could see the unshed tears in his SEAL's eyes. He had never seen him cry before.

Bryan walked in. "What are you guys looking at?"

"Kyle moved his leg," Shaw said in a hushed tone, as if afraid to say it too loudly in case it might vanish.

Bryan raced the last steps to Kyle's side.

"I didn't do it on purpose," Kyle told Bryan. "I don't know how I did it."

"That's okay," Shaw said. "This proves the nerves are connected and messages are getting through again. Can you move your foot?"

"I can try." Kyle concentrated on his right foot and felt his toes move slightly. "They moved."

"I saw them through your sock," Bryan was quick to say. "What were you doing before your leg moved?"

"Behaving like a child," Kyle admitted, not so proud of his behavior. "Complaining about being restricted to the house."

"He was getting riled up for sure," Shaw confirmed, making Kyle feel worse. "Hey, no. No, I want you to get heated if this is the result."

Shaw didn't look upset at his behavior, so Kyle decided to let it go.

"Should we call your doctor or therapist?" Bryan asked, his excitement easy to see.

"No," Kyle said. "Let's wait to see if it continues. I don't want to jump the gun." What if tomorrow it's gone again? "We'll keep this amongst ourselves until we're sure it's here to stay."

"Whatever you want," Bryan said.

"What about Fletch?" Shaw asked.

"Especially him. If he believes I'm going to be able to walk again, it'd kill him if it didn't happen." He knew his brother held some guilt about not finding Kyle sooner, and he didn't want to give him hope if there was none.

"Okay, we'll wait until you're sure," Shaw agreed.

"Thanks."

His men always had his back, and as he wiggled his toes a little more, the three embraced. Their private celebration was all he needed.

***

Shaw

Shaw walked out onto the back deck to find Gunner cleaning his rifle on one of the picnic tables. He was in the process of detaching the upper and lower receivers and wiping everything down.

"Hey," he called as he came over to sit down. "How's it going?"

"All's quiet around the ranch."

"That's good, but I meant how are things with you?"

"Fine."

"Do we have to play this game? How are you really, and why aren't you still with teams? I thought you weren't ready to step back yet?"

Gunner set down his cloth and looked Shaw in the eye. "Unforeseen circumstances forced me not to re-up when you guys got out. Now I'm trying to find a place for us to settle down."

"Us?" Shaw asked. As far as he knew, Gunner was single.

"Yeah, me and my nephew, Ben," he said with a small smile.

"You're caring for your nephew?" That was new.

"The unforeseen circumstance was my sister's death," Gunner said in a darker, deeper tone.

"Oh shit, Mandy? I'm sorry, man. I didn't know. When? Why didn't you call us?" Questions swirled in Shaw's head at the unexpected news.

"A week after you guys cleared out. A car accident." He said it as if he'd had to say the same thing repeatedly, which he probably did.

"Where's Ben?"

"He's staying with my aunt until I can get us settled someplace."

Someplace? "I can't think of a better place than right here. You'd have all of us to help out, and there's plenty of room at the lake house along with a job for you. He'd have a great time here on the ranch. Julia has a young son named Sammy, and I'm sure they'd be great friends. How old is he?"

"Four, and he still hasn't figured out why Mommy isn't coming to pick him up. I've explained it in simple terms, but he refuses to believe it," Gunner said while dragging the palm of his hand down his tired face.

"It's gotta be hard on the little dude and you. You lost your sister. If there's anything I can do to help, let me know. The three of us are always ready to help out." Shaw knew the others would feel the same way.

"Thanks, bro. I've already checked out the local schools and met the sheriff, considering he's Fletch's man. It looks to be a good place for a boy to grow up. Not too far from the cities, but far enough to be considered country."

"Hill Country, to be exact."

"Hill Country?"

"Yeah, this entire area. From west of Austin and north of San Antonio. About thirty thousand square miles before you hit the plains. The hills are mainly limestone and granite and rise about four to five hundred feet. There are lots of green trees and brush, and not a chain restaurant to be seen. The diner makes a way better double cheeseburger than any processed patty any day."

"Okay, okay," Gunner laughed. "I get it. It's a wonderful place to live. You sound like a real estate agent."

"I think it'd be the right choice if you stuck around, and that's all I'm going to say about it." Shaw didn't want to pressure him, but...he did.

Gunner smiled wide, reminding him of the man he knew back when they were on the same team. It was obvious he'd been through hell, and Shaw wanted to help him.

"I'll have to decide soon because my aunt's not able to keep him much longer."

"You could move into my room at the lake house, and there's an empty room beside it for Ben. I can't believe Brick wouldn't have already told you this."

"He did. Everyone did."

"Then whatcha waiting for?"

"I don't know. A sign or something from my sister this is the right move."

"I can't help you with that, buddy. Unless you consider my suddenly changing my ways and committing to not only one but two men as a sign or a fucking miracle."

"Hell, Mandy used to say when it was right, you'd settle down."

"Smart lady."

"Maybe it is a sign?"

"Feel free to use it. As long as you put down roots right here, I'll be your sign."

They both laughed as Gunner went back to cleaning his rifle. "I'll keep that in mind."

Shaw hoped his friend did. He'd be the first to admit when he arrived in Marshall, he wasn't overly impressed, having lived in the city most of his life. Looking back on it now, it was the best decision he'd ever made.

That'd make a great town sign. "Welcome to Marshall, Texas. Give Us a Chance."

CHAPTER TWENTY-ONE

Kyle

Kyle heard a noise, but he wasn't sure what it was. It sounded as though it was coming from below him. He opened his eyes and carefully leaned over the side of the bed to find a pair of pretty, dark brown eyes staring up at him.

"Aren't you adorable," Kyle said as he turned his body to face the sweet yellow lab puppy. "Where'd you come from?"

He looked at the doorway to find both his men and Isaiah smiling from ear to ear. They'd gotten him the puppy he was dreaming of, and he could feel tears gathering in his eyes.

"Our newest family member couldn't wait for you to wake up to say hello," Shaw explained, his voice light and happy.

"Her name is Gracie, and she's all yours." Bryan chuckled as the three drew closer to the bed where he'd been taking a nap. He'd been taking naps to beat the boredom. He was fully clothed. He threw back the comforter to uncover his legs and sat with his back against the headboard.

Shaw reached down and picked up Gracie so she could rush across the bed into Kyle's waiting arms.

"She's beautiful." He laughed as she licked his face like he was the best-tasting treat she'd ever had. "Where did you get her?"

"Well, there's a bit of a story behind that," Shaw said. "She's not only an adorable puppy, but she's a service dog in training."

"She's super smart," Isaiah agreed. "Watch. Gracie, sit."

Sure enough, the puppy plunked her butt down as her tail continued its frantic pace, and her tongue hung out the side of her mouth. Gracie was adorable, no two ways about it.

Kyle was aware of what a service dog was, and at first, he bristled at the idea of needing help, but the look of joy on his men's faces had him looking at it another way. When Gracie was fully trained, she'd help provide him with more freedom. Even if his legs began responding again, he'd need help at times. She was an adorable ball of love, and he didn't want to let her go.

"Will she have to leave for training?" Kyle asked as he hugged Gracie close. It would suck if she had to go away.

"No, she doesn't have to leave. Gracie will be trained locally along with you," Shaw said, coming to sit on the bed beside him. He always seemed to know what he needed.

"Me?"

"You. You're going to need to learn together for Gracie to have a chance to reach her full potential," Bryan stated as he joined them on the bed.

Kyle looked down at his new puppy, who'd calmed and settled in his lap. "As the only female in this group, she'll be running the place in no time."

"Damn right," Isaiah agreed. "Good to have someone else around here than you three lugs."

Kyle rubbed the top of her soft head. "Looks like we have a fifth family member."

"Welcome to the family, Gracie," Shaw said in a cheerful voice that made Kyle smile even wider. "I love you guys."

Kyle turned to look at Shaw as he heard Isaiah's wheelchair retreating down the hall. Bryan looked ready to burst while Shaw looked a bit stunned and unsure.

"I love you too. I love both of you," Bryan blurted out. "I've loved you two for a while, but I didn't know if it was too soon to say anything."

Kyle reached for their hands. "I love you, Shaw. I love you, Bryan."

Shaw's face cleared, and the three hugged as Gracie watched from her spot on his lap. This right here was a family, along with Grandad, Fletcher, and the team. The family he'd never known he needed, but would die to protect.

***

Shaw

There hadn't been any sign of the strangers in over a month. Everyone was beginning to suspect it might've had nothing to do with Kyle and Seattle. Slowly they'd been pulling back on patrols and allowing Kyle more freedom around the ranch. He'd even had Missy out for a ride around the barns.

The sheriff and his deputies had checked the entire county for anything suspicious and came up empty. All signs indicated they were clear to resume their normal routines, and Shaw had to admit perhaps they'd jumped the gun.

"Are you guys all set?" Bryan asked as he came up behind Shaw, wrapping his arms around him. He'd never get tired of that.

Shaw leaned back into his lover's body, enjoying the feel of being able to show his emotions without holding back out of fear. His men gave him that in spades.

"Yep. I'm waiting on Kyle and Gracie. Then we're off to our first puppy class."

"I wish I could come with you guys," Bryan said, and Shaw could see the guilt in Bryan's eyes.

"We know, but you have to be here when the vet arrives." They were doing pregnancy checks on the cows in order to separate the pregnant from the not pregnant for market.

"Can anyone join in?" Kyle asked from somewhere behind them.

They broke apart, and Shaw said, "Only you."

Kyle's smile was electric and made Shaw's heart jump. Gracie was riding on Kyle's lap as he wheeled himself over to the passenger door.

"Did you set up her doggie seatbelt in the backseat of the truck?" Kyle asked as Bryan opened the back passenger door.

"Sure did. Gracie's as safe as the two of you when you're buckled in."

"Thanks," Kyle said. "We don't want her getting hurt if something happened."

"Nothing's going to happen," Shaw said while lifting Gracie into the backseat and attaching her seatbelt.

He'd keep his family safe. He'd move heaven and earth for them. Looking back only six months ago, he was a completely different person, and no matter how in control he'd felt back then, he could see now it was a smokescreen for what was really going on.

Bryan scooped Kyle up out of his wheelchair and set him on the passenger seat. "I'll miss you, but have fun," he said before kissing Kyle.

"Wait, I want to show you both something," Kyle said.

Shaw came to stand beside Bryan outside Kyle's door. Kyle looked down at his right foot and moved it from side to side, his smile wide.

"Holy shit," Shaw said in shock. "You can move your foot now, not only your toes."

"That's amazing. I knew you could do it," Bryan added with excitement. "You'll be moving your entire leg soon enough."

"I don't want to assume anything, but maybe," Kyle said.

Shaw couldn't wait a moment longer before hugging Kyle close. Every day he was reminded of how strong and courageous his man was. As soon as he released Kyle, Bryan stepped in and did the same.

"We're proud of how hard you're working on recovering."

Shaw stowed the wheelchair in the truck bed before taking his place in the driver's seat. "We should be back home before supper." Then leaned over to kiss Bryan. Everything felt so natural between the three of them.

"Okay, drive safe, and I'll see you at supper," Bryan said before shutting the passenger door and stepping away from the truck.

Shaw started the engine and reversed out of his parking spot. "Ready?"

Kyle glanced into the backseat before turning to him and nodding. "We're ready."

Shaw put his truck into drive and began their journey to the neighboring town of Lansing, which had a satellite office for the service dogs in training. Today would be their first introduction into training, and he had no doubt Kyle and Gracie would be pros in no time.

Kyle played with the radio until he found a station playing rock 'n roll oldies. Perfect. Their windows were down, allowing the warm breeze to fill the cabin as they sang along to CCR and Bob Seger. Nothing could destroy this moment, or so he thought.

The first hit came from the back of their truck, and Shaw cursed himself for not paying closer attention. In the rearview mirror, he could see a black SUV with tinted windows getting closer to make another hit. Thankfully they were on a long quiet stretch of road, so no one else was at risk.

"Who is it?" Kyle asked in shock. "Was it an accident?"

Shaw dug out his cell phone and handed it to Kyle, who was holding on to the handrail above the passenger door while staring at Gracie in the backseat. He'd never been more thankful for a seatbelt in his life. Without it, the poor puppy would be sliding all over the seat.

"Call for help," Shaw said as he sped up. "This is no fender bender. Hold on tight. I'll try to lose them."

It was obvious the strangers had been biding their time, lying in wait out of sight until Kyle came back out to public places. Assholes were persistent as the SUV slammed into their rear bumper, almost causing Shaw to lose control of the truck. They fishtailed across the road, but he had the truck back under control and sped away.

"Help," he heard Kyle say. "There's a truck ramming us." Then Kyle gave their location.

Since Kyle had gotten hold of somebody, Shaw's job was to hold off the tangos until the team arrived. He cut off the SUV as it tried to pass them. The last thing they needed was for them to block the road up ahead. Kyle was quiet, and Shaw didn't have time to reassure him as he concentrated on the road.

They jockeyed for position as Shaw swerved across the road to cut off yet another attempt to come up the side of them. He'd be damned if he made it easy for them to take Kyle and pushed down on the accelerator.

The road had been mainly straight. Up ahead there was a small curve, and at the speed they were traveling, it might be enough to send them off the pavement.

Another hit had Kyle yelling out. "Assholes, leave us alone. Give me your gun."

"What?"

"Give me your gun so I can fire at them," Kyle shouted.

"Have you ever shot a gun before?"

"Ah, yeah. Have you met my brother?"

Shaw removed his Glock and handed it over. All this time, and he'd never thought to ask Kyle if he could use a gun.

The SUV managed to inch up beside him, and Kyle aimed the gun out the open back driver's side window. The first shot missed, but the second took out the SUV's rear passenger side window.

"Nice shot," Shaw said as the SUV backed off, allowing them to get several yards ahead before they reached the curve in the road.

"They're not taking me back," Kyle yelled.

"No, they aren't," Shaw growled as he sped toward the curve. "Hold on tight for this corner."

Kyle turned to face forward as Shaw slowed slightly to take the turn. They were halfway around the curve when they were suddenly hit in the rear quarter panel of the truck bed, throwing them off balance and sending them careening into a farmer's cornfield.

"Shit, hold on," Shaw hollered as the gravel sucked his tires farther away from the pavement. The squeal of rubber stopped as they went airborne after hitting a small culvert in the ditch. The world spun outside the front windshield, ending with them landing on their roof.

The last thing he remembered hearing was the crunch of metal, Kyle's scream, and Gracie's painful squeal. He'd failed at the one thing that mattered, and the people he loved would pay the price.

CHAPTER TWENTY-TWO

Kyle

Kyle could feel hands grabbing at him, and he fought with all he had, but it was useless as he felt himself being lifted out of the truck. Shaw needed help, and he prayed the team found him and Gracie in this cornfield. He realized he'd never see his men again, and just as he fell back into unconsciousness, Kyle hoped his death would be quick, and without more torture.

When he woke, he found himself in the last place he'd expected: the hospital. Why would they take him to a hospital when they were sent to kill him? This made no sense. The room was dark, but he could make out a lone figure sitting hunched over in a chair at the end of his bed. Kyle couldn't make out who it was, and tried not to wake them until he had a better handle on where they'd taken him.

He tried to push himself up using his arms and immediately cried out in pain. *Shit.* The person's head jolted up, and they sprang from their seat to take Kyle into their arms.

It took a few seconds, but the words finally made it through Kyle's haze of fear.

"Kyle, thank god you're awake."

"Bryan?" Why would Bryan be here? Did they take him too?

"Yeah. It's me. You have to be careful. Your wrist is broken."

"What happened? Where's Shaw?" Is he okay?" Kyle scanned the room again.

Bryan gently laid Kyle down onto his pillows and placed his injured hand on a pillow at his side.

"Shaw wasn't there when we reached the crash site."

"Did you check the cornfield? He has to be out there."

Bryan's eyes seemed to harden. "He was taken."

"What? Why would the people from Seattle want him?"

Bryan cupped the side of Kyle's face. "It wasn't men from Seattle. It was men sent by Joven Cruth."

Kyle searched his memory for the familiar name until it hit him, and his stomach fell. "The guy who wanted to take over Moroso from the Maas family?"

"Yeah." He'd never heard Bryan's voice so cold.

"How do we know for sure?" Maybe they took the wrong guy.

"They left one of their men behind. He'd been shot."

Had he hit someone when he shot at the SUV?

"Is he dead?"

"Yeah. Guess they didn't want to be riding around with a body in their truck. He's been identified, and the team thinks Joven doesn't want to hide his involvement as a lesson to others who get in his way." Bryan looked ready to explode. "The team is out searching for Shaw."

"I killed that man," Kyle mumbled in shock.

"The man they left behind?" Bryan asked, his dark eyebrows scrunched together.

"Yeah. Shaw gave me his gun, and I shot at the SUV. I thought I'd only busted out the window, but apparently not." Kyle wasn't sure how he felt about killing anybody. Even a man who worked for Joven. Though the guy was a known terrorist who tried to destroy the people of Moroso and wanted to kidnap Shaw.

"What about Gracie?" Kyle suddenly realized another member of their family was missing. "Please tell me she's okay."

"She's on the mend. The vet said she'll make a full recovery from her sprained leg. Gracie is waiting at home with Grandad."

"How long have I been unconscious?"

"Nine long hours."

"Any news on if they're getting closer to finding Shaw?"

"Nothing yet, but they'll find him. I know they will."

Kyle needed Bryan to hold him, so he lifted the covers on the side of the bed where he wasn't hooked up to an IV. "Please."

"You never have to try to convince me, love," Bryan said as he rounded the foot of the bed, took off his boots, and carefully slid his body onto the mattress. Kyle adjusted without moving his wrist, and with his man's help, his head was on Bryan's broad chest.

"Everything's going to be okay, right?" Kyle knew he was asking the impossible. Until the team found Shaw, there was no way of knowing. Hot tears slid down his cheeks and onto Bryan's button-up shirt.

"I have faith in Shaw. He'll find his way back to us."

***

Shaw

Shaw wasn't sure how long he'd been unconscious, but it was dark outside. Dumb to leave the windows uncovered and close enough for him to get a bead on where he was. He'd been tied up and left alone. It was obvious Kyle was never the target. It'd been Joven all along, but the motive was the same: revenge.

When they'd pulled him out of the truck, they'd held guns pointed at Kyle's head and told him if he didn't come peacefully, they'd shoot Kyle. He walked to the SUV without a fight, knowing the team was on their way to help Kyle, who was breathing when he left. They'd tossed the dead body of one of their comrades on the roadside. Typical terrorist playbook. Foot soldiers were disposable and easily replaced. They weren't concerned about being tracked. They figured by the time the dead guy was ID'd, Shaw would be dead and they'd be long gone.

Joven was waiting for him in the SUV. Shaw recognized him from the pictures Spence had shown him. He looked to be in his forties, with dark hair and soulless eyes. "This is the American hero?" Shaw remembered him laughing as they pulled away, and he was jabbed in the neck with a needle, which knocked him out.

He was awake now, and he had to get back to his family.

The room he'd been thrown in wasn't much. Eight by ten feet and looked to be an old office. His hands had been tied behind his back, making it difficult for him to open the drawer on the desk, searching for something he could use, like an old envelope opener.

No such luck. The drawer was as empty as the room with its lone desk and no chair. Or was it? Shaw could make out the edge of something metallic underneath the crumbling drywall. As he moved closer, he realized it was the metal support structure for the walls. Instead of using wood in the wall's construction, the builder had used metal.

It didn't take much for him to work the drywall loose until he had a sharp piece of metal to work with. Shaw turned around and began rubbing the ropes they'd used to tie his wrists against the sharp metal. Soon he began to feel fibers of the rope breaking as he increased his speed.

One, two, three more passes against the metal and the rope let go, allowing Shaw to remove it easily. He looked for a way out that didn't involve the only door in the room, and when he looked up, he saw it. The walls weren't constructed to the ceiling. They went maybe twelve feet up before open space led to the rafters.

That would be his way out. In no time, he scaled the wall in silence and moved over to the far end of the warehouse, looking for a way out. He passed by round two-foot vents bringing fresh air into the building, which he used as portholes to get a lay of the land.

He had no idea where he was. Nothing looked familiar. Then again, it was night. Several guards were stationed around the building's perimeter, making a clean break impossible. Shaw moved from one rafter to the next, staying in the shadows as much as he could. When he glanced over to his left, he saw a toolbelt hanging from a random beam. One contractor's forgetfulness was his possible salvation.

He hoped there was something in there he could use as a weapon because sooner or later, they'd discover he was missing. All he needed was to take down one guard, then he'd use their gun. When he looked inside the toolbelt, he found exactly what he needed. A hacksaw.

Shaw unscrewed the blade, removed it from the saw, and used an old rag from the toolbelt's side pocket to wrap around one end of the blade so he could use it without cutting himself open.

He came up to another vent and looked outside, trying to decide which side of the structure had more cover. He wanted to make as clean a break as he could. His goal was to put as much distance between here and freedom as he could, as quickly as he could.

Shaw thought he saw movement in the shadows of shipping containers, and he stopped to take a closer look. Then he saw it again. It could be the moon shining on some random piece of metal lying on the ground, but he didn't think so.

He lifted the shiny steel hacksaw blade to the vent and angled it so that he could catch the rays of the moon before sending out his team's call sign. He waited ten seconds and did it again. This time the response was immediate. Timed flashes in a certain order told him who this was, and Shaw was surprised it wasn't his team.

Dante and Spider had a crew made up of every military branch. They worked out of Brighton, here in Texas. Shaw had worked with Vincent and Shadow before. Brick must have called them in to help with the rescue, meaning his team was there as well. He loved the camaraderie between the armed forces. One of their own needed help, and they all came charging.

Knowing the state of play, he had to lay low long enough for the teams to get in place.

"Where the hell is he?" a voice roared from the other end of the building before he heard a single shot fired from the direction of the office where he'd been tied up. "Find him now, and don't disappoint me like that asshole did."

"Yes, Joven."

That confirmed the psycho had shot one of his men for allowing Shaw to escape. Small flashes of light had him replying to the teams he was all right. Hearing the gunshot had them concerned.

He could hear men running below and in and out of rooms as he moved above in the opposite direction. As long as he didn't alert them to his presence, none of them looked up. Poor training. While crossing from beam to beam, he'd stop to look out the air vents where he was sure his friends were preparing to attack.

His gut was killing him, and he was sure his captors had reinjured his gunshot wound. If he made it out of here with only that injury, he'd count himself lucky.

The next step he took guaranteed it might not be possible to come out of this relatively unscathed. The screech of an angry barn swallow sounded the alarm and revealed his hiding place. As the bodyguards' heads and guns turned up, Shaw saw Joven walking toward a side door as the power was cut.

The crashing and smoke assured him the teams were breaching the exterior, but Shaw could see Joven heading away from the scene in the moonlight. He had excellent night vision and had spent most of his career working in the dark. Gunfire went off below him as he saw a set of metal stairs leading down to near the same door Joven had exited.

There was no way in hell Shaw would allow that murderer to get away. When his boots touched the ground, he headed out the same door and directly into the path of one of Joven's bodyguards.

"Think you're getting away?" the man growled as he raised his gun.

Out of the corner of his eye, Shaw could see movement, and moments later, the bodyguard was lying on the ground.

"There you are," Fletch said as he came to stand over the downed man. "You good?"

"Better now. But Joven is getting away. I need a gun."

Fletch removed his handgun from its holster and handed it to him. "Take this."

"How is Kyle?"

"Broken wrist, bump on his head, and they're keeping him overnight at the hospital, but that's the worst of it."

"Good news. Gracie?"

"Sprained leg. Recovering."

The moment he had the most important bits of personal information, Shaw took off at a run in the direction Joven had gone with Fletch on Shaw's six. He could hear his teammate sharing their location with the rest of the teams.

They came to an opening between two shipping containers, and as soon as they attempted to turn the corner, a hail of bullets rained down on them. Both pulled back in time and doubled back to try another way forward.

Helicopters lit up the ground with their spotlights, making it easier to locate Joven, who was running alongside another warehouse. It was obvious they'd taken him to some sort of industrial dock filled with cargo and buildings.

Shaw and Fletch followed him until he ran inside one of the smaller buildings. They split up and entered through separate entrances to surround him. Shaw pressed his back up against the wall as he inched his way down one of the hallways. He could hear footsteps to his left, followed by a thud and groan of pain.

Shaw followed the sound to the last room on the left, where he stopped and listened.

"Do join us, Shaw," Joven said from inside the room. *Damn.*

He opened the door slowly, never once lowering his gun, to find Fletch was on his knees in front of Joven, facing Shaw. Blood dripped down the side of his head from where he'd been struck.

"You okay, man?"

"Be better once you put a bullet in this asshole." He looked more pissed than hurt.

"Shut up," Joven growled before bringing down the butt of his gun to the back of Fletch's head. Thankfully, he had a thick head, and it only made Fletch angrier.

"Drop your weapon, or your friend here dies."

"Don't do it," Fletch stated calmly.

Joven pressed the barrel of his gun to the side of Fletch's head. The look in the crazed man's eyes told him the fuckwad was a hair away from pulling the trigger.

"You shoot him, and I shoot you." Make him think about it, giving the others time to find them.

"You think I fear death?" Joven laughed. "I'd give my life for the cause."

Okay, maybe not. "What cause? Your quest for power is as self-serving as you are. You don't give a shit about your people and what's best for them. How's Bing, by the way?"

"Who cares. He was a means to an end."

"How does anyone in their right mind follow you? If you're not abandoning them, you're shooting them."

"Their deaths are for the greater good."

"Your greater good."

"I'm out of patience," Joven said before jamming the barrel harder against Fletch's head.

"It's okay," Fletch said. "Gunner sends his regards."

At that moment, Shaw noticed Fletch still had his bone mic on under his long hair. The others were speaking to him, and their sniper was in place.

Shaw smiled and lowered his weapon.

"Stupid American hero. Now you both die together. You should never have involved yourself in Moroso matters."

"Good-bye, Joven."

The man gave Shaw a strange look and was about to say something when Shaw heard the tink of the bullet going through the window's glass pane and straight into the side of Joven's head. Fletch stood without assistance, confirming he'd be fine.

"That's what you get, you fuckin' asshole," Fletch stated as he shoved the body away, "for coming after one of us."

"Thanks for keeping my six, bro."

"Shit, I couldn't let anything happen to you. My brother would kill me."

Both laughed as the building filled with the team members charging in with Brick and Dante in the lead.

CHAPTER TWENTY-THREE

Kyle

The next time Kyle woke, it was morning, and there were two men in his hospital room. He rubbed his eyes to make sure he wasn't seeing things, and the moment he moved, so did they. Bryan came out of the shadows, followed by Shaw, who looked a bit worse for wear, but wonderful all the same.

"Shaw," Kyle said in a hushed tone, too afraid he was still dreaming to speak any louder. "You're here. They found you."

"I never had a doubt the team would find me and bring me back to my men," Shaw said as he leaned over Kyle's bed and kissed him. The sight of him and Bryan confirmed everything was going to be okay.

Without thinking, he raised his hands to touch Shaw and feel how real he was when he was reminded of his broken wrist and hissed in pain.

"Easy," Shaw said as he gently placed his casted hand and wrist down on the bed. "I'm not going anywhere. No need for any sudden movement."

"Are you hurt?" Kyle asked.

"Other than a few bumps and scrapes, I'm all good. You're the one who has broken bones because of me. I fucked up when I failed to protect you."

"Failed?" Kyle asked in shock. "You didn't fail at anything. Had someone else been at the wheel when we were rammed, I doubt I would've gotten away with only a broken wrist."

"I'll try to remember that."

"You'd better. I won't have you disparaging the man I love," Kyle said with a smile. "On to a more important matter. When are you two breaking me outta here?"

"When your doctor says it's safe to do so and not before," Bryan stated. "You were found unconscious, and there's a bump on the side of your head."

"Okay, then which one of you is sneaking Gracie in?" If he couldn't go to her, she'd have to come to him.

Shaw and Bryan looked at one another with matching grins.

"I'll be the lookout," Bryan said.

"I'll handle the deployment of the puppy," Shaw stated.

"Does this operation have a code name?" Kyle asked, getting into the fun.

"Pupdrop," Shaw said without missing a beat.

***

Bryan

Bryan drove Kyle to the mansion where the women he'd helped save lived and learned while starting their new lives. They'd dropped Shaw off at the lake house on their way by so he could help Gunner and his nephew move into the team's house. Everyone seemed happy about Gunner's decision to stick around and put roots down here in Marshall.

"I wonder what the women want to talk to you about?" Bryan asked. "Since getting you out of the hospital, it's been go, go, go."

"I'm sure things will calm down soon, and the doctor confirmed I'm healing nicely," Kyle said. "What I'm hoping they want to do is talk about my offer to go into business."

"It's a great opportunity you're giving them, on top of all you've already done." Kyle's philanthropic outlook would see a great many things accomplished. The man was a miracle worker.

They pulled up to the imposing house, which had been made softer by new colorful curtains and flowers planted all around. Bryan jumped out and pulled Kyle's wheelchair out of the truck bed. He brought it over to the passenger side and in no time had Kyle in his chair and on his way up to the door. With his healing wrist, moving himself around was a definite no-go.

The door opened before they even knocked, revealing a smiling Alejandra waiting inside. She must've been watching for them.

"Hello, Mr. Daniels and Mr. Murray," she said as they neared the door. "It's wonderful to see you both again. Will Mr. Shaw be joining us?"

"No, he's down at the lake house helping a friend move in," Kyle explained.

"We'll be sure to pack extra food for you to take home to him," she offered.

"He'll appreciate that," Bryan said as he pushed Kyle through the door and on into the kitchen.

The rest of the women were cooking or waiting for them to arrive. The whole house smelled of food and spices, making Bryan's stomach growl. It didn't matter what they were cooking: he wanted a double serving.

The table wasn't set traditionally. There were two seats at the long table and various loaves of bread, tortillas, tacos, bites of food, tamales, flautas, and what looked to be fresh homemade tortilla chips. Pots bubbled away on both stoves, and bowls were being filled.

"Please sit and relax," Alejandra said while motioning to the chairs, which were for him and Shaw. Kyle rolled up to his place setting. "We have decided to consider your offer to start our own business."

"That's wonderful," Kyle cheered. "I can't wait to get you all on the road to success. What sauces have you decided to start producing first?"

"That's where we're having a problem. We can't narrow it down to two or three, and we hoped you two could help with that."

"I'd be honored," Kyle agreed.

"Count me in," Bryan added. "I could never say no to anything you ladies cook."

"I'm sorry Shaw won't be able to taste the sauces with us. It's an important moment," Kyle said and prompted Bryan into action.

"Ladies, if you want an even bigger poll of which sauces are your top three, we should have the team come over," Bryan suggested. "Military men know a thing or two about good food, and I'm told Gunner's a chef."

Alejandra turned to the rest of the group to discuss the possibility. Bryan was right. More opinions would help them decide.

"Thanks," Kyle said, and Bryan replied with a smile.

When the women were finished talking, Alejandra turned around with a huge smile. "We would love to have the team's vote."

Bryan stood. "I'll make the call."

The moment Shaw picked up, he asked, "Miss me already?"

"What if the answer was yes?" Bryan asked out of curiosity.

"Then I'd say good to know since I miss you too. How's it going?"

"Well, we need you and the team over here for some serious research. The ladies have decided to take Kyle up on his offer, but they need help to decide on the top three sauces."

"They're cooking?" Shaw asked, and Bryan could swear he could hear him salivating.

"Yeah."

"We're on our way."

Bryan knew it wasn't going to be a hard sell. "They're on their way," he said as he re-entered the kitchen.

More chairs were brought in for the team, and plates with cutlery were set out. The ladies set out small bowls of various sauces and *moles* in front of each seat, and beside each was a letter of the alphabet to keep everything straight when deciding.

He heard vehicles pulling up moments before the doorbell rang. Bryan stood and went to answer the door.

"That was fast," he said as he swung the door wide open for the team.

"Wouldn't want you to start eating before we got here," Spence said as he headed straight for the kitchen. Since Rick introduced healthier foods into the lake house, the man seemed perpetually hungry.

"Hey," Shaw said as he stopped to kiss Bryan. "Kyle excited?"

"He's over the moon."

"Great. With Kyle teaching the ladies about the business, they should be successful in no time," Shaw said as he took hold of Bryan's hand.

"Considering my brother has already created and sold businesses for a substantial profit, I have to agree," Fletch said as he walked in, followed by Sheriff Cooper.

"Elias, aren't you supposed to be working?" Bryan asked.

"Fletcher called and said there was help needed."

"I said the ladies needed help deciding on which products to sell," Fletch said with a laugh.

"That is not what my stomach heard," Elias replied.

Gunner and his nephew, Ben, walked in next, and Bryan could see how shy the young boy was even in Gunner's arms. Knowing the team, Bryan doubted it would take long before Ben ran the lake house.

As they all made their way into the kitchen, they took their seats around the table. Shaw bent over and kissed Kyle before sitting in the chair opposite him. They'd begun this configuration at home and when out. Bryan on one side of Kyle and Shaw on the other.

The team quieted down as Maria handed out pieces of paper and pens. The page had numbers and a line.

"Thank you for being here to help us," Alejandra said. "On the pages, we would like you to put a letter of the top three sauces beside the corresponding number."

Bryan respected how Kyle did none of the talking, choosing to have the ladies take the lead. This was their future. They deserved to have control over it.

"You're drooling, Spence," Rick said with a scowl from across the table. "You already ate this morning."

"We're here to help, and I want to help."

Rick rolled his eyes and turned away, but it didn't stop Spence from loading his plate.

When Shaw had told him about those two, he had to admit they didn't seem to be a match. There had to be something that drew them to each other. Bryan knew better than to judge. If a year ago someone told him what his personal life would look like today, he would've laughed his ass off.

It wasn't long before the colorful, fresh, smokey, spicy, savory, earthy flavors took over his senses. There were no two ways about it: these ladies were sitting on a gold mine of talent. As he looked around the table, the more the team ate, the happier their chefs seemed to be.

After every bite of food was eaten and the sauces were tasted, the judging began. The ladies stepped out of the room to allow the team to discuss their results in private.

"Seriously, can't we simply produce all the sauces?" Fletch asked. "They're so tasty."

"I have to agree," Gunner said. "This is some of the best Mexican food and sauces I've tasted."

Bryan looked over at Kyle, who seemed ready to burst. "You okay?"

Kyle broke out into a brilliant smile. "They're going to be so successful no one will ever take advantage of them ever again."

Shaw reached over and pulled Kyle into a hug, and Bryan joined in.

CHAPTER TWENTY-FOUR

Shaw

Shaw sat back and watched as Kyle cuddled under the covers. He knew his lover had something on his mind and he waited for him to get it out. Bryan, however, wasn't as patient.

"What's up?" Bryan asked as he pulled Kyle closer. "You look like you've got something on your mind."

Kyle looked between them before saying, "I want to be in the middle."

Shaw was confused. "You are in the middle."

Kyle shook his head. "Not now," he huffed. "I want to be in the middle when we make love."

This would be the first time Kyle had chosen their positions and Shaw was all for it. "Sounds perfect. Which ends would you like us on?"

He smiled when he said, "I want to suck on your cock and feel Bryan inside me."

"Your wish is our command," Bryan stated with a grin.

Shaw reached for the lube as Bryan and Kyle kissed. His cock was hard as a rock and the thought of Kyle's mouth and tongue on him almost made him blow.

When Bryan pulled back, Shaw took over, placing the lube into Bryan's hands before taking over the kiss. Kyle tasted of mint toothpaste, warmth, and love. His body shook and he moaned, confirming Bryan's fingers were lubing and stretching him.

Shaw made sure to keep his lover occupied and distracted by licking his way up Kyle's neck on his way to his ear and laving it with his tongue. Kyle's moans confirmed he was comfortable and into what they were doing.

Shaw leaned back and shifted his body up the bed to line up his cock with Kyle's mouth. Without a moment's hesitation, Kyle's tongue darted out over the head before moving closer to run his tongue up and down Shaw's shaft.

His eyes rolled to the back of his head when Kyle swallowed him down his tight throat. He was in complete control as Shaw laid his head back and enjoyed the attention. His moans flowing freely as Kyle's tongue worked its magic, running the length of his shaft, while his hot, wet mouth stretched around it.

Shaw opened his eyes and watched as Bryan's fingers entered Kyle. The look of concentration on Bryan's face assured him that every care was taken with Kyle's virgin ass.

"Fuck, your hole is sucking me in."

Kyle mumbled something, but with Shaw's cock in his mouth the hum served to send vibrations through his cock, making him cry out. The sight of his shaft sliding past Kyle's lips as he sucked him down was almost too much to watch, and yet, he wanted more.

He heard the tear of a package and turned to watch Bryan roll the condom down his long cock in preparation for entering Kyle. They'd agreed to get tested to do away with the latex barrier since they were in a committed relationship.

"Pull off, Kyle, while Bryan slides in. You'll need to breathe through this part."

Shaw slid his body down and took the top half of Kyle's body into his arms as Bryan lined up his cock.

"You ready, Kyle?"

Those striking blue eyes looked up at him with complete trust. "Yeah," and Bryan edged in. Kyle's eyes widened and he sucked in

172

a breath as Bryan moved slowly inside him. It took a while before he bottomed out and remained absolutely still as Shaw held Kyle tight.

He looked at Bryan, who was biting his bottom lip and blinking slowly. Maintaining control had to kill. Shaw asked Kyle, "Are you okay?"

"Oh yeah," he said as he pushed back a little.

Bryan's smile was instant, as he withdrew slowly before thrusting in again. Kyle's moans were a sure sign the man was enjoying what was happening so Shaw positioned his body for Kyle to have what he wanted. He grabbed Shaw's cock and drew him in with a slick pull.

With every thrust, Kyle's moans vibrated against Shaw's cock as he sucked harder. Bryan groaned, and as they seemed to be moving in tandem at an increasingly fast pace, Shaw knew he couldn't hold out much longer. His hips bucked in time with Bryan's thrusts, and Kyle's blunt nails dug into Shaw's hips.

"I'm going to come," Bryan gasped as he reached around Kyle and began pumping his cock in time with his thrusts.

Kyle pulled off Shaw's cock and cried out as he came; Bryan joined moments later. Shaw wrapped his hand around his cock and after a couple strong pulls, he came all over Kyle's chest.

"Holy fuck," Bryan groaned.

Shaw chuckled and ran his hand through Kyle's hair. His head lay heavy against Shaw's thigh, as sawing breaths brushed against his balls.

***

Months later

Shaw watched the play of emotions on his lovers' faces. They'd spent the last two hours expressing their need for each other in various pleasurable positions and were now lying in each other's arms as the moon shone in through their bedroom window.

"Do it again," Bryan said.

"Yeah. Do it again," Shaw insisted.

"C'mon, guys, I've been doing it all night."

"We promise not to ask again. Tonight," Shaw added.

"You guys are insatiable."

"You weren't complaining earlier." Bryan laughed.

Kyle huffed and said, "Okay, but only for the two of you."

He held on to both his and Bryan's arms for leverage before lifting up his right leg at a forty-five-degree angle. Shaw's emotions were all over the map. He was in awe of Kyle's perseverance and can-do attitude.

"I'm so happy for you." Shaw's voice cracked. Another new thing in the multitude of changes being loved by two men had brought him. He almost laughed at the thought of being a commitment-phobe. He didn't fall in love with one guy. Selfish to the end, he had to have two. With a mental shrug, he understood the bounty for what it was. A gift he never expected.

Bryan's eyes looked damp, but Shaw wasn't going to call him on it. Kyle had been working hard since he'd first started moving his toes. They'd convinced him to go to the orthopedist, who prescribed PT three days a week. Kyle worked his exercises every day, and he was beginning to see serious progress. He wanted to be standing by the time they attended the National Dips and Sauces Competition in New Mexico at the end of the year.

Walking was going to happen, but not by the end of the year. Kyle had a long road ahead of him, but Shaw knew his lover had a warrior's spirit. Kyle would get there. Shaw was sure of it.

Good things were happening for the ladies too. They were making a name for themselves and had the beginnings of a healthy following. They'd been selling online and at farm markets over the past seven months, and by all accounts, they were a success. A small grocery chain had approached them about carrying their products.

"Soon, I'll be getting a walker," Kyle told them before lowering his leg.

"I'm sure you will when you put your mind to it," Bryan agreed. "You are capable of anything."

Shaw pulled the sheets over the three of them as they tucked in. Bryan and Kyle soon fell asleep, leaving Shaw alone with his thoughts.

What a difference a year made. He'd been certified single for so long he barely recognized the man he'd become. And it wasn't a bad thing. Before, he had to worry about only himself; now he had a family to worry over, but he also had a family who loved him and worried over him.

Trust. Shaw had little to no trust in anyone outside his team. Now that circle had widened and included Bryan and Kyle and several individuals from the Marshall community. He held no fear of being betrayed by his lovers, which gave him an even more secure feeling than when he was alone and closed off. He never thought that would be possible.

Did he miss being single? Bryan's muscled arm reached across to cover the two of them while Kyle adjusted until his head was resting on Shaw's shoulder.

Hell no.

His life was so much richer. With friends and family ties, he stopped seeing himself as a loner. Sure, he could charm anyone out of their pants for a night, but it was an empty existence. He could see that now.

He'd gone out on missions since Joven's attack and missed his lovers like crazy while he was away, but his homecomings were all the sweeter. Bryan had even managed to get him out on a horse for the occasional trail ride. Kyle took to riding like a duck to water, and Missy was his chosen mount even though he had progressed enough to ride larger and faster horses.

Gracie was on her way to becoming a star in her own right. Service dog training couldn't have gone any better. She took to the lessons and became Kyle's third arm and legs when necessary. She especially loved to run alongside Missy when they were out for a ride.

At times Shaw would catch himself wondering if it was all real. Whether he'd wake up and he'd be back in his bunk guarding a patch of sand or in a South American jungle.

But all it took was a touch from Bryan or Kyle to bring him out of it.

They belonged to him, and he belonged to them. It was as simple and complicated as that, but he didn't want it any other way.

***

National Dips and Sauces Competition, New Mexico

"I'm so nervous," Alejandra said as the group of women milled around their section of the exhibition area. "I might be sick."

Maria walked over and hugged her. Shaw could see the pride on Kyle's face as they waited for the results of the competition. The group had three sauces up for awards: their *salsa verde, salsa roja*, and *mole poblano*. As far as Shaw was concerned, they'd already won.

The *Mujeres Guerreras* Company had placed third for their *salsa verde* and second for their *salsa roja*. All that was left was the *mole*, and they'd already announced the third and fourth place winners. Now they waited for the name of the winner and runner-up.

The day the women had agreed to Kyle's plan to make them business owners had been the start of something wonderful, and the company name they chose fit them well. Warrior Women, *Mujeres Guerreras*. They'd helped convert one of the outbuildings at the mansion into their processing facility and test kitchens. They didn't do large batches, making them even more unique, and the orders were piling up.

The twelve women shared responsibility and praise as their authentic Mexican sauces began popping up in stores across Texas. Laura and Crystal, the pair who took care of the women who'd been trafficked, had been added on to the business at the other women's request. As they said, the older women had helped rescue them, and they wanted to take care of them for a change.

Watching them begin to soar made Kyle all the happier, and now here they waited. A win would put them on the map.

"Are you okay?" Shaw asked Kyle.

"No. Yeah. I don't know. I'm excited."

"You sure you want to keep standing until the announcement?" Bryan asked.

Kyle adjusted his grip on the walker while giving Gracie a scratch behind her ear. "Yeah. I want to be standing for this."

Shaw's new life was filled with hope and happiness, and he wouldn't change a thing. He felt like anything was possible with his men at his side, along with Gracie, the wonder dog.

The judges stepped up onto the stage, and the room went silent. The women held on to each other as the judge holding the blue and red ribbons stepped up to the microphone. A jar of their *mole pablano* sat on one side of the table, with their competitor's entry on the other.

"Come on, blue ribbon," Shaw chanted.

Bryan and Shaw were holding on to Kyle's arms in case he jumped from excitement.

Shaw never imagined being this comfortable in his skin. Who knew moving to Fire Lake would be exactly what he'd needed?

"And the winner is..."

ABOUT THE AUTHOR

M. Tasia is a M/M romance author who lives in Ontario, Canada. She's is a dedicated people watcher, lover of romance novels, 80's rock, and happily-ever-afters (once the MCs are put through their paces, of course), who grew up with a love of reading. She's a firm believer that everyone deserves to have love, excitement, and crazy hot romance in their lives. Love should be celebrated and shared.

Connect with M.:
mtasiabooks.com
FB: mtasiabooks
twitter: @mtasiaauthor
IG: @m.tasia.author
TikTok: @mtasiauthor

www.BOROUGHSPUBLISHINGGROUP.com

If you enjoyed this book, please write a review. Our authors appreciate the feedback, and it helps future readers find books they love. We welcome your comments and invite you to send them to info@boroughspublishinggroup.com.

Follow us on Facebook, Twitter and Instagram, and be sure to sign up for our newsletter for surprises and new releases from your favorite authors.

Are you an aspiring writer? Check out www.boroughspublishinggroup.com/submit and see if we can help you make your dreams come true.

Love podcasts? Enjoy ours at www.boroughspublishinggroup.com/podcast

Made in the USA
Columbia, SC
19 October 2022

69699240R00107